BOY FROM SAINT-MALO

BOY FROM SAINT-MALO

SHIRLEY BURTON

HIGH STREET PRESS

HIGH STREET PRESS
Calgary, AB, Canada
highstreetpress.com
shirleyburtonbooks.com
First printing 2020

Printed in the United States of America, Canada, and worldwide under license.
Available in eBook formats.
Design and editing Bruce Burton
Cover art – Simpson, Charles Walter, 1878-1942, Canadian artist, 'Saint-Malo 1534'. Bibliothèque et Archives. Canada C-001956. Public domain.

Burton, Shirley, 1950-, author
        Boy from saint-malo / Shirley Burton

Issued in print and electronic versions.
ISBN 978-1-927839-27-0 (pbk.). —ISBN 978-1-927839-28-7 (hardcover)
ISBN 978-1-927839-29-4 (ebook)

"And above all, watch with glittering eyes the whole world around you because the greatest secrets are always hidden in the most unlikely places. Those who don't believe in magic will never find it."
—Roald Dahl, *The Minpins*

From the days of Genesis, we have depended on the celestial heavens and the magnetism of the moon to rotate the earth. Even prior to the bronze age, stars guided the astronomers in calculating journey distance as told in the New Testament of the three wise men following the star to Bethlehem.

Roman civilization became the basis for studying astronomy and astrology while Greek mythologies introduced the gods of the Sun as all-powerful to make the world revolve and aspire. Fascination with these tales inspires creativity and adventure to its limits.

The ancient Book of Thoth dates to when scribes recorded events in hieroglyphics, an early form of etching warnings painted onto walls of tombs. Later papyrus scrolls were collected by scribes. The mythical fate of these records being encased in a golden box at the bottom of the Koptos River passed down in ancient times.

The Book of Knowledge is an analogy of data and theories retrieved from all the great and powerful men in history. Gaeten Mansart, the boy from Saint-Malo is the instrument to demonstrate the internal unleashed power and ability inspired by the visionaries of Limoilou, the home of explorer Jacques Cartier.

The transformation of dwarfs, nymphs, serpents, and dragons is purposeful to express the degrees of power influencing Gaeten's generation and symbolic to his inner self.

When the elders and sages, visionaries of the past and future, bestow a spell of super senses on the boy, he becomes a believer in himself and opens his mind to his natural senses. Galileo is an astronomer studying the constellation; Copernicus studies theories and logical thinking; Aristotle is the guide to wisdom; Magellan is the fortitude of believing in the unknown; Puccini represents the greatness of music; Leonard da Vinci opens the eyes to the world of art. Gaeten is closely aligned to the voyages of Cartier to parallel his thirst for adventure and to fulfill his dream of being a mariner. From the crow's nest of Cartier's ship, the Grande Hermine, Gaeten travels to the new world and discovers his true fate.

Gaeten, an orphan, ages throughout this story from ten years to an adult. The people that interact with his life are portrayed as amiable and caring helping him demonstrate how he removes negativity. The mission is to seek potential, overcome barriers, value morals and protect himself.

This young mariner yearns for guidance in those he has admired. During the early 16th century, the belief in spells and curses is waning while extraordinarily personal power and determination inspired discovery and progress.

The colorful tales created in Greek mythology gravitate to the far corners of our minds. Leviathan and Ickty are transformations of both Gaeten and Ruskin, the offen, who have used their internal resources to overcome challenges.

The story of a young adventurer that finds his own rainbow and journey to believe . . . the spirit in all of us. My motivation to write this adventure is to inspire youth and adults to raise their barriers and seek their inner selves.

Shirley Burton

CONTENTS

1

Finders Keepers

As the morning sun breached the horizon, a lad climbed down the Saint-Malo fortress wall and skedaddled over the breakwater peninsula to the shimmering sand that chased the sea's tidal pools. A fiery-orange sunrise pierced the horizon with distant silhouettes of ship masts.

The shoreline divvied the northern French provinces of Bretagne and Normandy with the Channel islands following years of battle from the sea. Surrounded by a stone wall, the town stood far above the water.

Low tide peaked at 6:30 a.m., exposing an enduring beach dotted with strands of seaweed and windswept, sandy dimples, with keyholes denoting the presence of clams burrowing in the muddy beds.

The young blonde boy, Gaeten, wore a knitted beret and was barefoot, suited to his spirit of adventure. Scaling above rocks he knew like the backs of his hands, he scampered and slid over the seaweed slime, dodging the washed-up debris. His agility was remarkable, with callouses and scar-toughened feet molding his deftness as a forager.

With a twist to yank the mussels out, a knuckle sliced on a crag, but he moved on, stashing the sea creatures into a canvas bag that cooled in a small puddle of Atlantic wash.

Tracking the routes of the clams and crabs, he rapidly harvested a sufficient quantity of delicacies for the day's catch.

Gaeten was not alone, as hobbles of wooden boats knew the advantage of the solar system's magnetism and the best opportunity to draw in their lobster traps. The lad had at least another hour before the great wooden sea beasts would ease into the bay, returning from new world explorations.

Spokes of decaying wood from a bygone pier were encrusted along the rocky peninsula, swelling not only with barnacles but shellfish and crustaceans, in particular, the bearded mussel. Rotting warships and intimidating black hulls of pirate ships had created a paradise for sea life.

As seagulls squealed overhead, the boldest one charged at a jumping fish, its easiest prey. Gaeten flapped his arms, as a devious pair targeted his bag of mussels.

"Begone, you buzzards!"

One of the lobster fishermen waved from a vessel plying the shallow surf. "Ahoy thar', Gaeten! I could use a hand here as my traps are caught in the tide."

The aged fisherman, weathered from life on the salty sea, wore a torn shirt, an oilskin cloak and a seaman's hat salvaged from pirates' discards. Over his shoulder was a leather lasso with hemp ropes rounded into a hoop. His toothy grin broke his scowl and the crow's feet at the corner of his eyes squinted into the blaze of the morning sun.

The brawny lad of barely ten years waved his acknowledgment and buried his tied sack under rocks imbedded in the sand. Soaking in a pool of water would allow the sandy grit to escape the shells, all the better for eating.

"Oui, Monsieur," he bellowed, then half-ran the long beach and swam the short distance to the lobster boat. The old man was fighting with his twisted ropes, fearing he'd capsize with his day's haul swept into the surf.

"Can you dive, boy?"

"What for?"

"My cables are caught below, and I can't pull them up. Be a good garçon and untangle this blasted mess?"

Gaeten's quick glance at the horizon still showed no sign of the returning explorers' ships. As far as he could see, the sea was calm and clear, sparkling like diamonds.

With barely a flick of his feet, he disappeared below the surface, and the fisherman held his line firm from the boy's tugging below. Gasping for air, Gaeten surfaced.

"I'll need your knife, Monsieur Gallipeau. We'll have to cut a cable that's caught on a chunk of a ship's anchor or canon. It's too bad, Monsieur, but there's no other way. I'll help you mend it later."

With the gutting knife, he plunged back into the menagerie, knowing the seabed well from adventures with his brother.

The era of plundering in the English Channel left wooden hulls to rot, allowing courageous divers to be rewarded with buried coins or saleable relics from the seabed. Today was lucky for Gaeten. Spying the ridge of a silver British shilling with the etching of Henry VII, he tucked it deep into his pocket.

He knew this particular hull and worked arduously under the water, aware of the danger with exposed shards of contorted metal that could cut away at any flesh that tampered with its sleep.

Gaeten righted the lobster traps and gave a final yank. The fisherman replied with two short tugs, then the trap gushed in its suction of bubbles to breach the surface.

"Come ashore later, and I'll pay you to mend my cables. I'm in much need of help." The boy and the fisherman had built an affable relationship in the surf and counted on one another during not-so-easy times.

The old trawler gave him his best grin, having long ago lost most of his teeth to chewing tobacco and from gnawing on leather. It was the first time Gaeten looked closely at his friend. Deep lines of experience and wisdom concealed the man's sunburn, and the ravages of arthritis contorted his fingers while his muscles wasted against his bones.

"I'll come to you ashore, Monsieur Gallipeau, and we will make the lines good again."

With a thumbs-up, the lad returned to his collections adding a pair of shy sand crabs to his stores. Quickly the morning sun dried his clothing and he was off to find a spot at the market to sell. He held firm to the secret of his pocket.

Saint-Malo, perched on the coast of Brittany, was an independent kingdom waiting to become a Duchy. Its formidable presence deterred attacks, as the French soldiers buttressed themselves along the ramparts with black powder, muskets, and canons.

While defending from invasion on the Celtic Sea and the Atlantic, France was defiant and rebellious under King Francis I, who showed relentless greed and an appetite for power and fortunes, even as the French coffers suffered.

The king regularly ranted, "France has the right to the new land it explores and its riches. Challenge the Italians, the English and the Spanish to stake the land along the rivers and coastline."

Following the pronouncement forty years earlier by Christopher Columbus, the Genoese navigator, that the world was round, a nations' race was sparked to conquer the wealth of new lands and the gateway of the Far East.

In 1523, Francis granted a charter to the Italian explorer, Giovanni da Verrazano, to stake claims on the northeastern coast of the Americas, the place the Basque Whalers knew as Newfoundland, and to explore the Gulf of Mexico. Meanwhile, explorations were flourishing for the Italians, Spanish, French, Portuguese, English, and Basques.

It was natural to Gaeten to pretend to be a soldier, and occasionally he watched the ocean with a made-up patch over his eye.

Sitting cross-legged in the market courtyard, Gaeten laid his canvas sack beside a bucket of seawater where the morsels bathed. If he didn't stake his spot early, there would be none left, and the merchants would shoo him away for encroaching on invisible borders.

Behind him, the vending stall of the Hunalt family displayed their exquisite wares of terracotta pots, tapestry rugs from China and India, and exotic teas and spices.

Gaeten and Monsieur Hunalt had an agreement, that the lad could lay his selling mat and sit his pails if he helped in the shop when it was too busy for Madame Hunalt.

The Hunalts were a humble family with five children under eight years, including tiny Angelique who took a shine to the two Mansart brothers.

Gaeten surveyed the market crowds for his younger brother Julien, a freckle-faced boy shorter than others his age but confident of a growth spurt at any time. The boys lived together over a crude stable provided by the livery keeper in return for nightly grooming of his charges.

Sauntering through the bustling marketplace, Julien found the temptation of fresh, creamy brie too much to resist. Angelique heard his shriek and raced to find Gaeten and her father.

"Come at once, Gaeten. Julien needs help."

From the center of the courtyard, Gaeten kept pace behind the merchant who was now dragging Julien firmly by the ear toward the stocks of the justice of the peace.

Julien was placed in the confines of the pauper head-stock, while the jailer prepared his ten lashes. In remorse, he begged forgiveness for the mere crime of being orphaned and hungry.

Monsieur Hunalt arrived at the stocks to stand beside Angelique as Gaeten arrived.

"Papa, you must save Julien," she pleaded.

Monsieur Hunalt had no choice in the matter as little Angelique held tight whimpering. His strong voice cut through the heckling crowd.

"Please, Sir, he is but a child and an orphan. The workhouses are overfilled and there is no need to punish the lad in this way. Whatever fine is required to the cheesemaker, I will pay. Julien will work off his indebtedness to me."

Julien's crying ceased and his eyes followed to the jailer hoping for mercy. After a prolonged negotiation, he was unshackled from the stocks on the condition that he make amends to Monsieur Hunalt. However, if caught again the consequences would be severe.

"Merci, Monsieur Hunalt," Gaeten said. "We are greatly indebted for your kindness and generosity."

He dug into his pocket and withdrew the silver coin he'd found in the sludge that morning. Standing tall, he offered the coin to Hunalt.

"Gaeten, where did you find such a coin? It has the head of Henry VII who is not well-liked in these parts. But indeed it has a precious value one can't deny."

Gaeten did his best to complete a manly negotiation, then offered his hand in a gesture of a gentleman's transaction.

"I was a lucky hunter in the surf. It now belongs to you."

It was well-known in Saint-Malo that Madame Mansart died in childbirth and the brothers were left to fend for themselves. Their father joined the French privateers' ships in the Caribbean and had not been seen for years.

Gaeten had long given up hope, but Julien clung to the dream of his father returning with riches.

Every morning departing the market, Gaeten hiked to the crest of the hill over the peninsula looking to Grand Be for the silhouette of a ship bringing back its tales of adventure.

Whatever the ship might carry, it brightened Gaeten's hopes that one day soon, he too could join his father's dream of being a legendary mariner on the Atlantic.

The Mansart boys were industrious with domestic jobs and merchants' errands, eking out enough for yesterday's loaves from the back of Castillon's Bakery.

In mandated support of the king's bakery taxes, the bakers colluded with each other to keep the price of a loaf of bread exorbitantly high to enable them to pay the royal share. Gaeten never haggled or challenged the baker believing that in his own way he was nobly supporting the king.

The brothers had earned their reputation as honorable peasants, never cheating or pick-pocketing. The rewards allowed them to roam freely about town gaining the trust of merchants.

Gaeten spread his morning catch on the granite slab. With his fingers, he splashed drops of cool water to make it most appealing for his regular buyers. Around on the cobblestone were the usual carts bartering their wares, with all the lanes claimed by merchants.

Through the rabble, he saw Julien running toward him, distinctive by his limp. The previous year, Julien was struck by a horse's hoof and left to mend without a doctor's attention.

"Gaeten! Gaeten! I'm certain this time it is Father."

Julien's face beamed with the hope that Gaeten rarely saw.

Patiently at every sunrise, Julien climbed to a parapet over the harbor and searched the horizon for corsairs and galleons, while Gaeten silently dreaded another disappointment for his young brother.

"Slow down, Julien. I have mussels to sell and can't come to the harbor yet. Why are you so sure father is on one of the ships?"

Julien tugged on Gaeten's tattered shirttails to come.

"I know it's him. Sell your mussels to the fishmonger and come with me. Three ships are heading to the docks on the lea side. If you won't come with me, I'll go alone. You'll see that I am right. I heard talk about the treasures from Brasil. Father mentioned Brasil once, remember?"

Julien was not four feet tall, with a dirty freckled face, straggly hair, but the brightest blue eyes like his mother. Three years younger than Gaeten, he was six or seven and relied on his brother and it was Gaeten who protected him.

"Julien!" Gaeten said firmly with authority. "Let's go to the fishmonger then, but you realize we will depart without much profit for today because of your impatience."

"I won't eat as much as yesterday, I promise."

Gaeten bartered smartly with the fish seller and departed without his sack of crab and mussels. The man smiled broadly, pleased with the fresh stock.

"Come back tomorrow, Gaeten. You be good to me and I'll be good to you."

Gaeten pulled his woolen hat down over his ears and took chase behind Julien who was skipping over the rocks leading to the harbor. Horses and their carriages impeded their jaunt as the townsfolk gathered near the pier.

From the hill's crest, they saw a trio of corsairs riding low in the water under the weight of their hauls. A crowd converged to see the returning crew, mostly eager to hear of the adventure.

"See, they are heavy with gold, my dear brother!" Julien called. "Father's share will provide us with a feast like no other."

It was customary for the crew of a privateer's ship to share a portion of the haul and many seamen along the coast of Brittany lived royally on arrival back in France, but later would hunger on the battlefields or awaiting the next ship.

The stinging stench of the harbor filled Gaeten's lungs, but he quickly became accustomed and turned his pleas to the arriving captains and harbor merchants.

"Monsieur, may I have work unloading your cargo? I am agile in small spaces and climb well."

His voice rose among the throng of locals of every age seeking hire and attracted the attention of Captain Antoine Mercier, commander of the ship Saint Phillippe, returning from the Carolinas.

"Yes, a child of your size will be useful," Mercer declared above the mob, pointing at Gaeten.

"Come quickly, boy or another will take your place."

Julien, unaccustomed to the work, followed his brother eagerly to keep up. "Where is Papa?"

"Do as I do, Julien, and we'll feast tonight from our own labors. Father is not aboard this ship!" Gaeten said with certainty.

In the crush of sailors and privateers, Julien gave up the notion of breaking away in search of his father.

"I'm too little for this, Gaeten. I'll get lost or trampled under the load."

"Quickly, Julien, there's no time to argue. Stay right with me."

Gaeten spoke with an authority his brother seldom heard. "You will only fail if your mind tells you so. You are not too young to do your best."

The first mate's eyes gleamed with the taste of superiority. Tucking his hand into his belt, he strode like a great eagle swarming over his prey.

"You two boys, get in the rafters and start hauling pelts. Go now and work fast if you expect to be paid."

The lads spent the day toiling in the stifling hold carting heavy sacks on their backs.

"See Julien, this is not Papa's ship. But indeed, it is heavy with gold as you say, and we will feast tonight, but not with our father."

2

Verrazano's Return

Days later, a trio of galleons returning from the Spanish islands and the Carolinas were barely visible in the Sea of Silon, but nonetheless gave reason for sounding the harbor bell. The sleepy town was awakened from its droll pace, as all the chimes rang out calling laborers, townsfolk, merchants, mariners, and even the local urchins to scurry to unload the ships.

The sound ignited excitement in Gaeten's chest, one that put him in drastic motion. With feet running, horses galloping and voices cheering, the town maneuvered toward the bay. This had happened a hundred times before for Gaeten, but the passion of the moment needing to win never faded.

A town crier announced the name of the returning ship, recognized by its distinctive mast and metaphor signals. She was an ornate galleon with seventeen canons and a sight to behold.

"Yonder is the Delfina, commissioned to Giovanni de Verrazano. Welcome back to France in the name of our king."

Gaeten mumbled his approval to himself.

"Certainly Verrazano is among them. His stories are legendary of the high seas and pirates. He will remember me and Monsieur Cartier too."

The queue clambered toward the rickety piers beyond the jutted boulders that made a natural erosion barrier. The furled masts were magnificent, and behind one, another young boy waved from the crows' nest.

Gaeten plotted as he grabbed his carpenter's tool belt and a hemp lasso. "Of course it is Verrazano's Delfina and thar' is young Telesphore, manning the topmasts. I shall ask permission to climb the crow's nest myself to check for needed repairs . . . any excuse to get aboard."

The great ship heaved and groaned easing her bulk against the pilings of the pier. Rugged outstretched arms and eager hands reached for the heavy ropes to twist around the anchor posts and marine bollards before they could lay a crude gangplank.

Gaeten was fixed on the lithe lad dropping from the masted beams of Verrazano's ship. "One day I shall be in the crow's nest, I know it in my soul. Telesphore will tire of the sea and I will be ready."

Clatter reared behind as a sleek, black carriage wheeled around him on the upper road from the Portneuf quarter, and all of a sudden the lead horses reared and whinnied.

"Whoa, boy!" Catherine Cartier pulled hard on the reins as she careened the stallion, then the carriage lurched forward back onto the road.

Long, golden tresses of curls wound up in layers on her head were covered today in a heavy bonnet. Cushioned on bustles of crinolines, she rode high on the front seat skillfully directing the team.

Gaeten recognized the carriage of Limoilou and recalled the first day he had met the lovely Catherine. It had been a day not too dissimilar to this morning a few years before when Verrazano's ship returned with her husband Jacques Cartier from Mexico.

On that day, the carriage had not yet come to greet the ship. Gaeten knew something was awry. The lady of the manor had lost control of her reins coming out of the paddock and the stallion was frantic bolting from the stables.

Courageously, Gaeten stepped in front of the stallion to calm him, staring directly into its fiery eyes, with its nostrils flaring, putting his own life in danger. Puffing and whinnying, the steed resisted.

"Whoa Sebastian, my beauty . . . whoa!" The horse and boy had stared each other down until the steed heaved with reconciliation. Gaeten pulled on the bridles, whispering calmly while breathing slowly into the horse's nostrils.

Occasionally since then, Catherine would send for Gaeten to help at Limoilou, in Cartier's absence. He enjoyed working in the garden, grooming the carriage horses, and making carpentry and wheel repairs. They never discussed the occurrence again but shared a respectful bond.

Jacques Cartier was esteemed in Saint-Malo, coming from an established family in royal favor. His own father, Jamet, knew his son would follow the passion for the sea and made sure Jacques was tutored in navigation. As a lad, he never missed the mooring of a ship returning to port then begged to view the logs.

From an early age, Jacques was considered a Master Pilot and drew the attention of Philippe Chabot, who was Sieur de Brion and High Admiral of France. Chabot extolled the young man's promise and skills before Francis I.

The Cartier family's prowess at sea and their staunch loyalty drew the attention of the king. After reviewing young Cartier's commendations, he was invited to join the crew of Verrazano on his sailings to the Caribbean.

Today, Gaeten's legs carried him like the wind in a footrace with other boys. The first indication of something seriously wrong was the flag flying today at half-mast. It was not Verrazano that disembarked as the captain.

"Mon Dieu!" Gaeten held his head with the shock of it.

Chatter swept like a wind across the throngs as the joy was displaced by sorrow.

A terrified crew member appeared at the first gangplank with his seaman's hat crumpled in his hands.

"The Captain was murdered in Guadeloupe by angry natives when our captain bravely went ashore to greet this newly founded tribe. Verrazano's brother, Girolamo, along with the apprentice Jacques Cartier chartered the Delfina back home. Our dead were buried at sea according to the wishes of a mariner."

His voice quietened as he solemnly crossed his heart and mumbled a prayer.

When Verrazano's grief-stricken brother stepped forward, the crowd silenced to hear him in a background of gulls calls.

"Giovanni loved exploring and it would have been his wish to be buried at sea. The remains were handled with honor as we gave him to the Lord's hands. I expect to see his vision rise over the waves the next time I pass that way."

Jean Le Veneur, escorted by another priest, came from the Abbey to give last rites and offered a prayer for the deceased Captain. Local mourners instinctively gathered for a solemn service.

Numb from the shock of Verrazano's murder, Gaeten halted his climb up the ship's ladder. He called to the crow's nest where the other lad smaller than himself was preparing to descend.

"Ahoy, Telesphore, wait! I am coming."

"Non, I must do my duty."

Telesphore ignored Gaeten and swooped to the deck in two swings from the mast. Seconds later, Gaeten was at his friend's side, assisting with the grappling hooks and canvases.

"It must have been horrible, Telesphore. I couldn't believe my ears."

"It pains me to speak of it. Mon Capitaine was taken quickly and the bloodshed was over in mere minutes. They desecrated his body and left him to the vultures. I try not to let my dreams come at night. The crew has spoken little of it on the return. Monsieur Verrazano's brother and Monsieur Cartier guided us back across the ocean."

Cartier beckoned to Telesphore to bring the logbooks ashore so he could prepare his report to the king of the cartography and day-by-day accounting of the journey and its achievements.

Telesphore scrambled to follow Cartier.

"I will find you outside Gravel's Alehouse later, Gaeten."

Catherine rushed to the side of Jacques as he set his boots back on French soil.

The crowd hushed and pulled back to allow the revered Cartier to pass.

As Cartier neared, Gaetan thought he was enormous in his great cloaks, beret and pointed beard. For an instant, their eyes met and Gaeten knew his world had changed.

Cartier gestured with his index finger to come as he tilted his head. "Gaeten, my boy."

"Indeed, Sir, how can I be of service?"

"Please assist Telesphore with the voyage journals and then rally at Limoilou directly. Monsieur Verrazano has family matters and his grief to attend to before he can join me."

Cartier scratched his head with a thought. "And the rolls of maps from my chambers aboard must be brought immediately."

"Of course, Monsieur Cartier."

Gaeten turned on his heels and swung himself up the gangway.

In haste, as he ran toward his friend, he neglected an overhead pulley hoist lifting an injured mare over the side of the Delfina.

With a smack and a thud, he was down, wondering to himself, "Why is Telesphore's voice becoming so faint? The masts are swimming over me soon to crash on my head. My body is numb, and I can't move, but I see it all. Those faces are staring at me so oddly."

It was Julien's panicked voice he heard first. "Gaeten! Gaeten! Get up."

Then the face and voice of an angel spoke to him. "Gaeten, don't move. We will have you lifted to Limoilou. No, no, no—don't try to get up."

She dabbed at the blood oozing from his head wound.

As Catherine hovered, Cartier ordered crewmen to lift the boy to the carriage and lay him gently on the seat. She kept his wounds wrapped in strips of cotton from her petticoat and patted a handkerchief on his face.

Mumbling in delirium, Gaeten repeated over and over, "I must get the maps. I need to get the maps."

3

Days at Limoilou

Limoilou Manor was a stately mansion with a stone terrace overlooking the Atlantic. Red tiled roofs and imported glass windows from Italy enhanced the grand two-story main house.

The manor could be seen from the town square rising above the forest, with a high garret, a solitary turret, and a thatched roof extension. Positioned on a terrace tripod, a telescope was trained on the horizon at sea.

Gaeten fell into a comatose state and lapsed into a vision of himself lying on his bed of hay in the livery rafters looking up through broken slats.

He could smell the barns below and hear the moaning of its occupants. The mumbling of sympathetic voices echoing his name was tormenting in his disorientation.

"Yes, I am at home. Can't they see that I am here?"

Absorbed in the magnetism of the heavens, he had his own window to the universe and its celestial phenomena.

Gaeten had heard talk at the harbor, of sea captains navigating according to the star of Polaris and reading the tides. His fascination with the stars and how they might rule the world set a deep longing in him for the experience.

Suddenly, as if in a dream, he opened his eyes to an apparition of the famed Italian astronomer Galileo himself, beckoning Gaeten to the giant telescope on a mount through the skylight.

Gaeten rubbed his eyes in disbelief. He'd heard of apparitions coming to great men destined to have inspiration and wisdom to change the world.

But I am a young boy.

He closed his eyes and opened them to discover Galileo still standing before him.

The aged gent insisted that he study the constellations and the magnetic pull of the stars that play with the ocean. The astronomer stroked his curly, grey and white beard, and his deep brown eyes penetrated the boy's thoughts.

"Isn't it magnificent, child? Polaris is the key to the rotation of our planet. You see, we are mere pawns in a masterful game of knowledge. Do you often watch the North Star?"

Galileo's eyes glistened with a hunger that inspired his curious and innocent mind.

"I was talking to Copernicus just now," Galilieo said. "It was about how *you* have been chosen by the stars. He thinks that the Sun rather than the Earth is the center of the universe.

Galileo laughed jovially. "But he comes from the Rennaissance era when emotions rule the mind. Myself, my revelations are yet to be but essential in the aspiration for great knowledge—a bit ahead of my time."

The astronomer wore a spectacular velvet and tapestry vest with a braided, rolled collar and an Italian, velvet tam that drooped over the tops of his ears. A lone monacle hung from a gold chain at his waist.

Gaeten thought it was peculiar that he could smell wine and sausage on his clothing, and his mind drifted.

Surely, in dreams, one loses the sense of smell, taste, and touch while in a stupor. How extraordinary. I recall a gentleman in the market who sold handmade flutes, in spite of being deaf and blind. His remaining senses overcame that and he played beautiful music. The senses are so magical.

With a strain of his muscles, Gaeten tried to sit up to see better, but his weak body failed and he slumped back onto his pillow, overcome with a swooning headache.

Where did the famed star watcher disappear to and where had he come from?

"Galileo . . . Copernicus . . . c'est impossible," he said in confusion. He returned to his fever but remembered the distinct appearance of the astronomer. The pain swelled like a tide in his head as he longed for the vision once more of the dreamer.

During the dark of night when the house was still, his eyes shot open at a brilliant light that glowed from across the room.

"The doorknob," he said. "Its lustrous beam is surging like an invitation for me to come."

Beyond the room, he heard footsteps, the kind when a person tries very hard to be unobserved. Remaining still and silent, he listened to tip-toeing in the halls.

"Someone else is awake! Where am I?"

Searching his surroundings, he couldn't make sense of the room at Limoilou or how to make his body move.

His legs wouldn't budge, but the power of the doorknob still beseeched his spirit. The light of the moon through the window sash lent enough to show him the floor. Whether he crawled, walked or drifted across the room, he didn't know.

Laying his hand on the knob, he felt its warmth flood through his body, then heard someone calling his name.

Welcoming whispers urged him on. "Gaeten, Gaeten!"

The brass knob rotated in his hand and a subtle creak let him know the door was opening. Voices were louder now, happy, chatting, and telling tales.

In the room was Galileo, talking with Copernicus and the great French artist, Leonardo da Vinci.

From his night vision, he knew Galileo at once, then the process of deduction identified Copernicus, a studious mathematician, with his attire precise and symmetrical. Long-bearded Leonardo, he recognized, as he'd seen him passing through Saint-Malo.

Overwhelmed with awe, he passed through the open door, but tripped over a rolling brass gyroscope, no bigger than what would fit in the palm of his hand.

As the contraption ricocheted in the hallway, the voices stopped and Gaeten saw more clearly the images of huddled miniature creatures surrounding him.

He knew of mythical little people in Aesop's fables.

Are these dwarfs, or the pixies of old childhood legends?

As tension lowered, humming and new chatter filled the chamber, with small magical animals roaming and behaving as almost human, uttering sounds in a universal language he'd never heard before.

An aged, grey sloth hung from the ceiling stretching in painful slow motion to reach out for Gaeten. Nearby, a miniature hippo was nudging a puppy to play ball. A nest of bald eagles was perched high up on an oak branch that protruded from the earthen walls.

The awe was overtaking him until a staccato finger snap diverted his attention. It was the man with the long, straggly, grey beard.

"Dear lad, we didn't mean to wake you. Usually, at this time of night, the house retires, and we go about our work."

"Are my eyes deceiving me? Are you truly the master, da Vinci?" the boy asked with a voice of respect.

Leonardo departed from his easel and laid his brush aside. He held out his hand with his gnarled, crippled fingers, and Gaeten felt it safe to inch forward.

"I beg your pardon, gentlemen, I didn't mean to intrude. The doorknob glowed and my curiosity was undeniable."

From behind, Galileo interjected, "Undeniable curiosity is the key to the universe, so make no apology. This is the door to wisdom and knowledge and a true understanding of the world."

Leonardo spoke at last, "Myself, I am relatively new to this sanctuary where great men deposit their gifts for the development and education of others. Although my body has faded, the intangible mind goes on in infinity. In the years to come, my art will be studied and offer an insightful view of expression and depth of color. It is my gift to the world. It is a sin to conceal knowledge."

"Although young in years, I understand," Gaeten said.

Leonardo nodded at the boy's youthful wisdom. His words expounded about his death seven years prior. Even now his hands were not idle as he continuously sketched those around him. Behind his easel, blueprints of inventions covered the wall, with designs and foresight that would astound the world as his genius would become known.

The smaller man, Copernicus, studied the boy's face. "They say you have a concussion . . . does it hurt?"

"I don't really know, my faculties are fractured and my memory is distorted. I must go and seek my brother."

Galileo consoled him. "Ah, that would be the boy, Julien. He was here this afternoon and is sleeping in the stables. Rest for now and all will be clear in due time."

Listening to the seers, Gaeten heard a voice that quietened to a whisper. "Julien is small and agile . . . almost the size of an offen, the dwarf-size little people you are certain to meet in time.

"An offen? Dwarf-size people? Will I know when I see them?"

"Yes, indeed, Gaeten. And we may need Julien to help us with the abyss. There's always the unknown, but he has determination and spunk to get back."

"Get back from where?" Gaeten asked.

"The body can only physically travel if it has youth and determination, Copernicus said, "but the mind differs, it is infinite. I see that as a mariner, you are a kindred spirit, ready to participate in the exploration and studies of the world. One must want more than he has to allow his mental resources to be maximized."

"I don't truly understand where I am or the objective of this gathering," Gaeten said. "But, yes, I want to know about the heavens and the earth and discover new things."

Leonardo nodded again at his childish insight. "First you must believe in yourself, boy. Think long and hard on that— every person has powerful qualities and resources. Don't look for the tangible, but the unseen. You may think you know us by our appearances, perhaps even our clothing, but you will soon see *that* is not the defining characteristic of each contributor."

Galileo's contented smile caught da Vinci's eye and he added, "Knowledge and learning are infinite and we are here to preserve that."

The heavy fog returned, and once more Gaeten felt the pillow under his head. Peering into the mist he could see the Delfina in the harbor and smelled the foul stench of the seaweed and dead fish trapped in the rocks as the surf washed over them. He knew the harbor, rock by rock, even through the mist.

Struggling from slumber, a faint, distorted apparition rose before him, but he couldn't move. He knew the man appearing, an officer from the Delfina, standing on the bridge calling toward Gaeten, who stood by the moorings.

"His eyes are upon me."

"Ahoy, Gaeten, I was hoping you would come. Hop aboard with your brother, lad, and lend a hand in the ballast."

Verrazano was relieved to acquire the services of the Mansart boys before the other two ships completed disembarking.

Girolamo Verrazano and Gaeten recognized one another from harboring in Saint-Malo, from the earliest days of the boy's thirst to be a mariner.

"Yes, Sir, permission to come aboard?"

"Why is there an unseen ghost standing behind you?" the officer apparition was startled to find himself in a dream.

The mouth of the corsair opened onto the dock and great wooden rollers came forth with bales of fur, cases of blubber, and Spanish pirate treasure taken from the Gulf of Mexico.

On deck, two mariners from the Delfina were bragging about the gold they had seen. "I was with Verrazano when I saw the banks of the Carolinas. The Spanish are preoccupied with the gold treasures of South America. The Brazilian gold was so heavy that the galleons sank before they were plundered."

The tallest slung a heavy bale of tobacco over his shoulder.

"Girolamo said to go to the Taverna tonight and we will get our share. Hush, I fear someone may be listening."

For a brief second, the world froze before Gaeten's eyes, then his memory flashed back to the accident, with the sight of the horses being winched into place. Before he gave the cargo a second glance, he saw Jacques Cartier coming from the master's cabin with rolls of maps.

Catherine tethered her carriage dockside and heaved her skirts from the carriage. Copernicus had heard the bells tolling and the household rush of Madame Cartier to get to the harbor. He was committed to the elders' decision—Gaeten would be the gifted child and they had a duty to watch over him.

Copernicus took advantage of Catherine's crinoline pockets and reduced his size to show not more than a pair of wizardly elfish leather boots. Secured out of sight, he waited, and at the moment of the hoist overhead, Copernicus peered out, awaiting his opportunity.

As a mathematician, he assessed the weight and distance to impact and made spherical alterations to minimize the injuries to Gaeten.

The hoist carrying the weight of Champion made an unexpected swing to the left, then Copernicus willed the rope to snap under the weight of the mare.

"Madame, he will be the one," Copernicus gushed.

His words impaled Gaeten's sub-conscience and his memory of this dream faded.

"I must get the maps as I promised I would," Gaeten mumbled into space.

The boy moved in and out of unconsciousness for several days, yet in his slumber, he looked forward to the nocturnal visits.

From time to time when Catherine peered in to check, she heard him whispering about the charts and Copernicus.

4

Secrets of the Slumber

Three days after the accident, Catherine eased her great hoops and crinolines into the sick room. There on the cot lay the small boy. In spite of her longing, she had not been blessed with children.

"I've heard that his mother died years ago and his father has gone afar to seek his fortune. He seemed so much bigger and older charging up the gangplank."

She stood watching him. "Ah, he is breathing better, more like a slumber."

Moving to the side of his bed, she stroked the tangled blond curls from his brow and spoke softly. Slowly he stirred and rubbed the sleep from his eyes.

"Gaeten, it is morning. I thought you might be hungry." On the nightstand, she placed a tray for him with porridge and cream.

"Where am I?"

He puzzled over the familiarity of her face. "Madame Cartier, did Galileo send you?" His eyes darted to the far wall where he had seen the door and its glowing knob, but he was dejected to see nothing but a plastered wall.

Amused by his comment, she smiled. "No, dear boy, you know me and you are recovering here at Limoilou. You will stay until you are strong. I'll let Julien know he can come to see you and that you are awake."

"I am sorry for the trouble I've caused. I should go back to the livery or my spot will be taken. Monsieur Devereau is strict about the chores being done."

Gaeten struggled to rise from his cot, but Catherine was firm.

"I went myself to Monsieur Devereau and assured him your chores would be done. Emmanuel, my chore boy, is happy to help and said that when you are better, he will square the debt. Julien is sleeping over our stables, he refused to come into the manor."

"You are too kind, but I am well enough."

The attempt to stand on his own was a failure as his legs buckled beneath him.

"Gaeten!" Catherine spoke with overbearing confidence. "We are indebted to you and will not feel our due until you are strong. You were helping Monsieur Cartier when the rigging of the hoist failed. Otherwise, you would not have been there."

"The hoist failed? All I remember was that I needed to get the maps. Mon Dieu, I have failed Monsieur Cartier."

"The poor mare was just as surprised but she landed on hay bales. My father was the chevalier du Roi and local constable; he gave Champion to my husband in my dowry. She is being treated like royalty in our barns. All is well."

Catherine's jovial voice was calming to his ears.

"But you see, Madame, I was born a mariner like my own father. When I sleep at night, I listen to the distant waves as the moon carries the ocean to Saint-Malo. I am certain that I hear my name in the wind."

"Dear Gaeten, is your father due to return to Saint-Malo? He will be surprised to see how you and your brother have grown."

"Merci, Madame. Julien believes that father was on the ships, but I fear another sadness for him. My brother clings to hope and the image of a noble man, but . . . " Gaeten turned away.

"It is your father's loss not to see what a fine lad you have become. I have taught myself that the sea is a disease that afflicts many men. The call of the ocean and the anticipation of discovery awakens their souls every day. Alas, I understand that is the heart of a mariner."

"Oh, indeed, I do, but Julien is too young to fend for himself. One day I will be worthy of accompanying the great masters of the sea to the new world. You see I have *undeniable curiosity*."

Catherine gave a pained smile of comprehension, then leaned in to whisper. "Listen well and learn more . . . the door will open again. I had my first contact when I was a wee girl in this very house. It is a blessing to be sure."

Surely she was not a party to the secret chambers! It would be rude to ask.

Gaeten looked at Catherine with awe then an understanding. Madame smiled as she rose, and it was clear that Gaeten had more questions.

"How old are you, Gaeten?"

"I don't know for certain, but I believe I'm about ten. Will the secrets disappear as I grow older?"

"Each person chosen is blessed in a different way. I am sometimes used to access knowledge and opportunity, but I have never spoken to another about what I have said here. You see, I have not the gift, but I have channels that prove invaluable. I have the opportunity to open doors when the seers need."

She gave a wink from the door. "Monsieur is preparing his report to the king about this last voyage. Do you read?"

"I have never attended the study halls or encountered a schoolmaster, but I hear from the tavern window and the harbor talk and understand the language of navigation. I read symbols from charts and maps. I know too that Polaris will guide a mariner wherever he is."

He looked up with hopeful anticipation. "I listen and learn, which is all the wisdom I am entitled to."

"Everyone is entitled to wisdom, but it is good to seek guidance. About Polaris . . . where do you hear such talk?"

"I lie awake on my bed at the livery and watch the stars. I know the heavens well."

"You are wise for a small boy."

"Every ship that comes to St. Malo has a story. Even the tales of long ago. I know about the Atlantic route and the voyages of John Cabot thirty years ago. The Tudor standard was planted on a place called 'Kahnawaye' near a settlement to enable trade with the Tuscarora natives."

Gaeten did his best to recite a conversation he'd overheard. "The king longs to see the fleur-de-lis planted by a French patriot. I know that white is for clergy, red for nobility and blue for the bourgeois."

Catherine raised her eyebrows in surprise.

"You are better versed than I am. When you have eaten your gruel and are strong enough to stand, I will see if it's possible for you to meet with Monsieur."

Catherine did a final exam of his bump and head wound before leaving, satisfied that the fever was behind. She opened the windows to allow the sea breeze to refresh the room.

Overwhelmed by his conversation with Madame, Gaeten forced his legs over the side of his cot. His legs responded as if he had never known how to walk, and the effects of gravity rushed to his head, leaving him with an imbalance.

Nevertheless, he forced the porridge past his lips and sipped the cream, satisfied to have something solid in his stomach. His unselfish thought went to Julien wondering how he was faring to feed himself.

On most mornings, Gaeten had gone to the back of the bakery to gather stale goods for the day. Otherwise, the earnings from his morning catch would buy soup bones from the butcher, watery gruel from the tavern kitchen, or a piece of fish cooked by Madame Hunalt.

"But this is the finest. I've never tasted cream before. Madame said that it was goats' milk from their own paddock."

From his bed, he looked out the window onto the slate terrace of Limoilou. Below was Monsieur Cartier, studying the ocean through his great brass telescope from its tripod base.

"Magnifique!"

He wasn't sure how long he had remained at the window when Monsieur Cartier turned to go into the manor. He looked up at Gaeten's face at the window and waved.

"Gaeten, if you are well enough, come to my library,"

"Oui, Monsieur Cartier."

He had always known where Cartier's library was from occasions when he was summoned to help Madame.

Leaning on the wall every few steps for strength, he arrived to find Cartier leaning over a grand, polished desk, with maps spread from corner to corner.

"I see you are up, Gaeten, but I do say you look awfully pale. Please sit here."

Cartier gestured to a chair beside the table. "Perhaps a stiff cup of tea will do you good."

Monsieur rang a brass bell that dangled on the bottom of a cord from the terrace draperies, and seconds later a maid arrived.

"Madame Casolier, be so kind as to bring strong tea and a bit of the medicinal cognac to fortify my friend."

Gaeten tried to stand and make a slight bow of gratitude to Madame Casolier.

"Merci, Monsieur Cartier."

Gaeten thought Jacques Cartier to be a giant in physique and was mesmerized by his every movement. Distinctly, his groomed mustache and pointy beard were unique and impressive.

Cartier studied the boy's face as if looking into his own soul. "My wife tells me that you have the makings of a mariner. I thought I'd like to see for myself."

"Yes, I *am* a mariner. I hunger for the sea and the secrets beyond for the thrill of discovery. It is not fortune that I seek. The sea is in my bones. A wise man told me that wisdom comes from listening and learning."

Cartier was intrigued. "Very insightful. You are well-spoken for your age. Gaeten, who was the wise man?"

"Would you believe me if I said it was Copernicus?"

Cartier burst into laughter.

"Don't let my wife influence you with her imagination. I've heard that the learned men visit my house, but I am unconvinced since they have not chosen to show themselves to me."

"It is extraordinary, but great minds hold the future of the world. It is the knowledge that we must follow, not an individual. Explorations of the new world are important for everyone."

Gaeten regretted that he may have sounded impertinent.

"It is good to want to follow your beliefs," Cartier said. "I too hunger for the sea and the unknown beyond." Once more he studied Gaeten. "Every voyage is not always successful, with the danger of not returning to St. Malo. Have you thought about that?"

"My brother Julien is seven years old but he knows that when I am twelve, I plan to follow my instincts of the sea. That's two years to teach him to fend for himself and rely on the good people of St. Malo to watch over him."

"That sounds bleak for Julien and you have forsaken your faith in our 'good people'."

"No, he will find his own calling, and I am teaching him how to be independent. He believes that our father may one day return from a voyage, but I feel certain that will not happen."

"You are remarkable for your age, Gaeten, and I have enjoyed our chat. I wish to show you something here."

The maps were spread out unrolled on the desk. The sea was concise with details and the topography of the landscape was equally meticulous.

"These are partially recorded by Verrazano, and the latter part was written by myself. You can clearly see the route the Delfina had taken. This was not my first voyage with Verrazano—eight years ago I charted for him to the Carolinas then we founded the New York harbor before going to New Found Land."

"You have been privileged in obtaining commissions."

Cartier's fingers ran across a dotted line.

"I must hand these to the king in a few days, but since you're a fellow mariner, I thought you'd like to see them."

A thrill ran from his toes up to tickle the hairs on the back of his neck.

"Merci! Ah Merci, Monsieur Cartier. This is more than I dreamed of in a lifetime."

Cartier crossed his arms over his chest and paced back and forth across the terrace door. Gaeten sat in silent awe taking in every detail of the charts. He was so enamored that he began licking his lips to taste the sea salt in the air while imagining the rollicking waves.

"Gaeten, I have appeals through our Abbott to seek favor for a commission of my own ships. The king insists that the Saint-Vincent Abbey make the recommendation, but these petitions take time. I could use an apprentice to study the maps and learn the navigation of the Atlantic."

Then he spun around with a glint in his eye to face the lad. "Would you be interested in learning to guide the crow's nest?"

Cartier seemed larger than ever as he stood face to face with his hopeful protégé. Gaeten saw great wisdom in those dark brown eyes searching his soul and gained new visions of standing on the bridge at the side of the explorer.

"I presumed Telesphore had secured that post, Monsieur."

"Surely you can see that the Delfina has two captains and only one crow's nest. When I have my own commission, Telesphore will stay on the Delfina. Does this interest you?"

"More than anything, Monsieur Cartier!"

"Ah, bien! You will come to the chateau at the end of every day and study my library, maps, and charts. And you will be in need of a mathematician to help you with your analyses and provide you with training so you can set navigation codes. Do you know of someone?"

Gaeten envisioned the elder men as his teachers.

"Oui Monsieur, I know of the best."

"Then seek out your teacher and come to me when you have an analysis that we can discuss."

In spite of his weak condition, Gaeten sprang from the chair and bowed in gratitude. He was anxious to return to his room and call for Galileo, Copernicus, and Leonardo.

5

The Great Teachers

Gaeten crept up the staircase to his cot in the garret. Scrutinizing the plaster wall, he only wished the three magicians would reappear. Closing his eyes tightly, he begged them to present themselves to him, but it was not enough.

With his ear cupped to the wall, he called out. "Galileo, Copernicus, Leonardo? I need to speak with you, please show yourselves."

For a long minute, there was no sound, then he imagined the shuffling of feet and stirring behind the wall. Stepping back, he stared as the foggy figment of the door reappeared and the doorknob began to glow.

In the background, a crescendo of noises caused the floor to rumble, but he had no fear.

He heard Leonardo's voice calling back.

"Gaeten, you must put your hand on the doorknob and turn it. You command your own destiny."

The brass knob was warm to the touch and he recoiled at the first grip. On the second try, he succeeded, but the creaking and groaning seemed endless.

It was Galileo that first peered out from behind the door. Beyond, to his astonishment was a commotion of other seers he hadn't seen before.

"Come in, Gaeten, we are delighted to see you again."

"And I share the delight, my esteemed friends," he answered, with a maturity beyond his years.

In the grand foyer, Gaeten's eyes widened at the whirr of activity as a pulley rotated from the ceiling with chimes and pendulums, and a fabricating machine weaved baskets. Across the cavern, a cauldron was boiling water while steam puffed through pipes creating a wind draft rotated crude turbines.

"Wonderous inventions—what a marvelous menagerie." Gaeten chuckled with glee and elation.

Overhead, an axle pivoted with giant wheels and gears, activating a contraption he'd never seen before. In the background, a conglomeration of technical equipment moved across a conveyor belt, transporting inventions too numerous to absorb.

The skylight was filled with astronomical devices and instruments, and in the center of the room, da Vinci's great canvased easel held a midnight indigo painting of the moon and stars with floating celestial beings, with the heavens as a hollow eternity.

Scanning the cartographer's stacked desk he turned quickly to observe Galileo's mathematical variations. A mechanical chair arrived on a metal track bringing the artist, da Vinci, with a brush in his hand.

"Your vision of the moon is magnetic, Monsieur da Vinci. I feel the power of its gravity over the oceans." Gaeten realized he was stuttering, intimidated by the master, and with the effect of the masterpiece on his soul.

"Merci, Gaeten. I have succeeded to stir your emotions. You will always look at the moon now with greater understanding."

Calculations were etched on another easel, and behind it, a fishermen's net held magical tools designed by great imaginations. Tall bookcases had dozens of cubby holes, with scrolled charts, and shelves of parchment documents and journals of Roman engineering and Biblical accounts of the Mediterranean. A railed track slid a ladder back and forth across its library shelves.

"Gaeten, we heard you have good news from Monsieur."

"Then you understand my situation. I am in need of mathematical instruction, and I could think of no other than the masters in this very house. I've never had the instruction of a teacher, but I will try my hardest."

"Indeed, we are eager to have a scholar, however, we have a quest in return."

"A quest for me? I am indeed honored, but unworthy."

The three great men closed in around Gaeten.

"Sit child, we have a tale to tell, one that has never been written." Copernicus pointed to the mechanical chair vacated by Leonardo, and Gaeten climbed onto it.

The magical chair began to spin around and around, but he was not dizzy as he could see his surroundings in spite of the velocity, and absorb knowledge at a remarkable speed.

Images swirled like a whirlpool around him—visions of birds and sea creatures, kings and conquerors, battlefield conquests, inventions, dinosaurs and mammoths, extinct animals, and dreams of progress.

An array of florescent nautiluses from the deep sea floated in a brilliant coral reef and he reached out for a shelled orb that brushed up against him. The mollusk was transparent silver with an aquamarine enameled shell. It was cold and wet and skimmed directly to his hand.

Suddenly the nautilus burrowed into his pocket, and Copernicus noticed its escape.

"Don't be afraid, Gaeten, the nautilus will reveal a message to you in its own time. Guard it at all costs."

"I feel like I have stolen something."

"No, the nautilus has chosen you," Galileo affirmed. "Always respect its power."

Behind a labyrinth of tunnels and caves exuded melodic whispering sounds, music so wonderful he couldn't concentrate on Galileo's words. His heart swelled with innocence, purity, and an appreciation without limits.

"The joy is miraculous!" he said over and over.

"Someone is attempting to put a distracting spell upon you, Gaeten," Copernicus suggested, nodding toward the hidden nautilus.

Gaeten felt the magnetism and tried his hardest to pull away from it.

"I don't believe in spells. This nautilus seems harmless as a token of beauty. But as you've instructed, I will learn to be respectful of its power."

The sages looked at one another with alarm. "There is more for you to know," Copernicus said. "But first, you must have a complete understanding of what the Book of Knowledge represents.

Galileo conceded. "Very well. Copernicus, you should explain the quest."

A solemn hush fell over the room with all eyes on Copernicus. "The keepers of the world have gathered for eons to preserve education and make way for progress."

"Are you the 'keepers'?"

"We are not the only ones or the first. Don't you wonder about the mysteries and myths of this world? Even before the pyramid texts in hieroglyphics and the Biblical scrolls, I heard it mentioned that Egypt's ancient Book of Thoth was the source of the world's wisdom, but that it also carried curses and evil spells."

Gaeten listened intently to take it all in. "Tell me more, Copernicus."

"An offen once explained that all of the offens were equal until a spell was cast on his ancient ancestors. The spell was carried forward in every generation turning them from handsome princes to ugly gremlins."

"Hush, Copper, don't say those words of evil here," Leonardo cautioned to the others' astonishment. "Gaeten, if anyone speaks to you of Thoth, you *must* get away from the person. Run and don't let your mind be tainted to that evil, but instead remember truth and beauty are in everything you see or imagine."

Copernicus nodded at da Vinci's wisdom and spoke again to Gaeten.

"If you wish more about that, we will tell you. For now, accept that the ancient records of the Book of Thoth were written on papyrus by an Egyptian scribe. Thousands of years ago, many battles were fought to recover the oldest papyrus. The original documents are sealed in a golden case within other boxes, buried at the bottom of the mythical river of Koptos. An evil chamber there houses serpents and scorpions, to prevent anyone from raising the boxes.

"Multitudes have tried in vain to obtain the papyrus excerpts. Then, hundreds of years ago, we were blessed to receive a wealth of Egyptian scrolls, but the underwater thief was cursed with damnation, and thus the scrolls as well.

"They are written in a language that is complicated to translate, however, we have worked tirelessly over the years. And that my dear friend, brings up to this moment." Copernicus sighed at the conclusion.

"What is it that you want from me?"

"You may think our story is unbelievable, but believe you *must* if you are to be successful. Gaeten, you are physically much smaller than we are. A lithe and agile boy of your sorts could maneuver through narrow crevices and wriggle into tiny caverns.

"Many eons ago, others were here and our group of elders became responsible to maintain the great Book of Knowledge with its secrets and ciphers."

Copernicus pointed to the huge, leather-bound volumes and papyrus scrolls on the high library desk.

"The Book of Knowledge is unfathomable. You see, centuries ago, an angry dwarfed fellow became part of our sanctuary . . . his name was Clovis. He boasted of being as old as Methuselah and claimed himself to be a rightful heir of the Prince of Kyoptos and therefore spared of the curse.

"Over a period of years, we noticed that the journals grew thin. Following Clovis, we observed him stealing pages in the dark of night that he took down the tunnel until he came to a crevice. With the rolled the documents in his coat, he slithered into the next cavern, with no one able to follow him. We carry the wisdom of the world in our minds, but our bodies are old and frail, it takes all our strength to transform."

Leonardo said, "I was not here at that time, but one of the ancient offens told me that Clovis read the forbidden hieroglyphic documents and it cast an evil spell. He became a crazed man and withdrew from his community, losing the capacity for logic and compassion. One can never afford to lose those traits and survive."

"Logic and compassion," Gaeten repeated. "I will remember."

"Using Galileo's astronomy lenses, we have been able to see beyond the entrance that Clovis took. The terrain is uncertain and hilly, but we can see the journal up high on a rocky ledge with the scrolls."

The boy tilted his head to Leonardo with a smile. "You want me to follow into the tunnels and retrieve the pages? Surely I am small enough to follow the footsteps of Clovis."

The three elders exchanged a pleasing nod.

Gaeten wondered about the mysterious absence now of the offens that the sages spoke of, and his mind continued with a torrent of queries.

"Where is Clovis now? Is he in the tunnels as well? Is he dangerous?"

He sought to remember details of this moment, of the forbidden document and the stories of Clovis. As they spoke, the hidden nautilus warmed in his pocket, and his courage was bolstered for the mission.

It would seem that the nautilus is not only my trusted guide but the holder of a spell. I have a thousand questions.

"Son, there are many things to tell you," Copernicus said. "As in anything in life, there will be good and bad, and we must make moral choices. We work to create inventions and understanding for the world, not accumulate gold for selfish greed. Clovis is conniving and determined to convert the knowledge and spells of Thoth into his own fortune."

Gaeten's eyes wandered to his surroundings, searching for an offen. "Are there others like him to watch for?"

Peering through a cobble hole were two identical nymph-like people that recoiled when he spied them.

At his tall desk, Leonardo rifled through an assortment of his sketchbooks. "Here is a drawing I did of Clovis, with an accomplice named Punket."

"They do appear very short," observed Gaeten.

"Yes, short in stature, and their knees come almost from their hips, that you would assume to be cumbersome. But truthfully, they were both exceedingly quick on their feet. Some common folks would refer to them as nymphs or gypsies, but to us, they are *offens*. Take a close look."

Gaeten leaned closely to study da Vinci's drawings.

"Long, crooked noses, and oversized ears with gold hoops," he said. "And their grotesque feet and hands . . . "

"Yes, four-toed feet with grips of a salamander and six fingers on each hand."

"He has a nasty scowl on his face . . . I would not trust or befriend such a man or creature."

"Do you believe in spells and curses, Gaeten?"

It was a question he didn't feel he knew how to answer.

"I don't know for certain."

"You will need to answer that question for yourself very soon, Gaeten," Leonardo urged.

"One night there was a great commotion in the hall where the offens slept," Copernicus said. "Somehow a clan of men invaded us . . . other offens, disgruntled for being ridiculed by society and rejected not for their intelligence but simply for looking different. The invaders dragged Clovis and Punket away. Clovis had an acute memory that could retain and recite anything he'd read, and folklore insists that he visualized everything he had seen or heard."

"Instead, Clovis whined and cried like a child begging us to intercede," da Vinci said. "They could have contributed so much and left an impact on understanding in the future, but it was for naught. Someday, when you are the captain of a ship, you will face the fear of mutiny and that is what happened here."

From the desk, Leonardo drew out a compass chain and a scrap of silk. "In the struggle, these were left by Clovis on the floor. The chain is pure gold with an etched marking on the tab, stolen from the royal courts. The silk piece has high-quality Persian threads, part of a tapestry serpent."

"Isn't a serpent a symbol of danger and evil?" Gaeten queried. "I once saw a Spanish ship come to the port with a gang of pirates bound and ready for jail. The Spaniards had saved them from a watery death at sea. A defiant one waved a flag with a serpent and a fiery dragon and spat, 'Death to the king.' The poor man was given many lashes for his deed and later hanged for treason."

Copernicus bragged, "I met Ali Baba in Arabia one time, and he had such a flag too. I'll say . . . he could cook up a story about his band of thieves and might hypnotize anyone with the serpent he carried in a basket. It was said if you looked in the eyes of that snake, it was certain death. I wouldn't want to be tested." He ended with the deep-throated laugh of a pirate.

Galileo waved his finger. "Don't mind Copper, he loves an audience for his tales. Many Greek myths tell of the powers of snakes—some good and others evil. All in all, we don't know what symbolism the serpent has."

"I'd be more worried about the king's constables catching me with a royal gold chain than a scrap of material," Leonardo said. "We have more serious matters."

"Many great men have come through here and still visit, inspiring those who remain," Galileo said. "Perhaps one day you will meet Aristotle, Socrates, Magellan or Puccini, and you'll be inspired by the senses that are untapped. In time, you will understand that language is universal."

"In foreign languages, you mean."

"Yes, but beyond words. Language is in nature, in animals, the constellations and in the ways we communicate with each other."

"For me, it is in my art," da Vinci said. "With Puccini, it is the magnificence of operatic music that will be revealed to a future generation, and for Galileo, it is the whole of the heavens. There is a sacred place on the thatched roof beside the warm chimney where we think and contemplate under the stars, where we can let our senses truly open."

"Oui, Monsieurs." Gaeten's eyes were wide. "Someday, I would like to go there."

"I must return to Madame and make my way back to the livery, but I'd like to return soon. Monsieur wants to make a mathematician out of me. I need instruction every day."

He grinned as a humble plea and Galileo understood.

"We have depths of knowledge or talents in different ways, but each is equally valuable to a young scholar. We will take turns instructing you. The next time you come, we will show you the tunnels and you'll see for yourself."

"Since I won't be in this very room, how do I find the door?"

"We have bestowed a special gift on you, Gaeten, and we will hear your call."

The three masters looked at one another with winks and nods. "Look at your surroundings in a new and different way—a door can be anywhere, maybe where a larder might be, where ships are, even where ale houses abound.

"Your senses are to be used for good to help another, to protect yourself, and pass on knowledge to us."

"I will never forget."

"And be assured we will always hear you, but you must believe in yourself. You will soon learn that we are omnipotent."

Galileo tucked a flute-sized telescope into Gaeten's ragged pocket. "This will bring reality into the night."

"You are certain that it is a gift and not a spell?"

"Trust in us as we are here to guide you. We will send you into the unknown with a challenge to seek providence for your country and your soul."

6

Return to the Livery

Gaeten's feet were heavy, not wanting to leave the enchanting world of the elders, filled with magic and knowledge. He was ready to know more about the new senses he was empowered with and to investigate the exquisite mollusk in his pocket. His eyes searched for a place to examine and secure the nautilus.

"I cannot lose such a treasure. It will be safer here in the house at Limoilou than in the livery."

His fingers ran around the corners of the door jamb, the chair railings, and wainscoting, then the kickboards encasing the floor, seeking something that would have some give to it. Then he saw a crack where the floorboards vanished under the corner boards.

Gently, he tugged at the board until it snapped and released without damage. Packing the nautilus in a burlap rag, he hid it behind the board and secured it.

"No one will ever know!"

He stopped in his tracks. "That is not true, the seers are omniscient, all-seeing and knowing."

Invigorated with his future prospects, Gaeten thanked Catherine profusely for the nursing care and hospitality at Limoilou.

"Madame Cartier, you must send for me anytime you need help with chores, as it will be my delight to assist. I will leave now to find Emmanuel on my way. Merci! Merci!"

He bowed as he backed out the door. "God grant you many blessings."

With her shawl wrapped about her shoulders, she lingered in the doorway watching him skip down the lane, back to his world. She knew it would leave an empty spot in hers.

Gaeten bounded directly toward Devereau's livery with a spring in his step, The rickety barns seemed different, with the bustle of merchants and esquires depositing their stallions and mares at the stable, giving him new urgency.

The sky was grey with drizzling rain and a chilly breeze, but he was seeing the world in brighter eyes and sharper senses. He closed his eyes to better take in the sounds and smells of the village.

By scent alone, I know where the ocean is, the bakery, the livery, the kitchens, and the perfume of women. I better understand the senses of sight, sound, smell, taste, and touch.

Letting exhilaration take control, he saw the lush hillside to be greener and heard the church bells echoing a soul-chilling hymn.

The cawing of seagulls was no longer ugly but beckoned a joyous discovery. The rhythm of carts and carriages was melodic, and the sound of a child playing a lyre in an upper studio brought him to laughter.

Gaeten let a delightful laugh rise from the pit of his stomach. "Ah, oui, I am apprenticing in perspective!"

Standing in the town courtyard, he lazily rotated a full circle with his face toward the sky, letting the gentle rain splash his face as he caught the raindrops. Feeling invisible, he hadn't taken in the folks bustling past him.

A bourgeois carriage ambled toward the town courtyard, directly in the path of Gaeten. As the clatter of hooves roared closer and closer, he swung around startled to face the oncoming charge.

"Out of my way, you filthy urchin!" the driver spewed with a crack of his whip at the boy.

Darting out of the way of the stallion pulling the coach, he caught a glimpse of Monsieur Boniface's fury.

The man wore a fine, long coat jacket with the frills of a lace-edged shirt and a distinctive horsehair wig of white ringlets under a despicable wide-brimmed black hat, festooned with feathers. But it was the heavily caked makeup and sweet lotions that frightened the boy out of the way.

Boniface pulled up his horses short and snorted his outrage to Gaeten. The Monsieur was well-known for a bad temper, and bystanders backed away lest he spews his wrath.

"Garçon! Take my horses and carriage to the livery immediately." Boniface swung down from his seat and turned abruptly prepared to strike. "Do it now, urchin!"

His face was red, interpreting Gaeten's slow reaction as insolence while thrusting the reins into the boy's hand.

Another snapping crack of his whip demonstrated his ire, and disdain ravished his face.

Tall, black leather boots with silver toe points were the first things Gaeten saw. Transitioning back to reality was a shock as he heard the man's threatening tone.

"What's your name, lad? I should report you to the Justice for rudeness. A few lashes in the stocks will make you take heed and show how to be humble before the upper class."

Crouching, Gaeten bowed in submission and apology. He reached for the loose reins to prevent the horse from wandering into the path of others. Hastily taking charge of the team and carriage, he headed for the stables.

"Merci, Monsieur!"

"Hmph!" Monsieur Boniface yielded. With a final snap of the whip at the feet of Gaeten, he turned and walked toward the silversmith's shop.

Leading Boniface's sleek stallions in a trot, Gaeten reached the livery in seconds. Monsieur Devereau had been watching his apprentice while polishing a carriage.

The crack to my noggin seems to have rewarded me with the gift of super senses. It is overwhelming.

Everything was loud—the merchants selling street wares, the carts and carriages on the cobbled streets, the butcher shop, the baker's stand, and the smell of roasting in the air.

"Good day, Monsieur, I have brought you Monsieur Boniface's fine horses and carriage." Gaeten winked at the irony.

Devereau gestured that Gaeten should take over shoeing the livery occupants, but was nonetheless glad to see his hire return.

"Monsieur Boniface is ungracious, but you did well to bide your tongue. Are you strong again? You gave us all a terrible fright."

Glancing at the boy and deciding for himself, Devereau rattled on.

"That is good that you brought me business as I am in need of a hired fee. Charlebois will return within the hour for the shoed horse."

"I'm glad to be back. My apologies for leaving you in need—the horse will be ready."

Devereau suddenly reacted to a second thought. "Julien and the lad came every day from Limoilou and did a fine job, but you and I better understand the order of things. While you were not in need of your bed, I rented it to an Italian mariner. I will send him away when he returns."

Gaeten felt saddened that his bed could not remain a few days without him for the sake of profit.

Relieving himself of Boniface's charges, Gaeten sighed and sat on an upturned wooden crate, realizing his senses were not only heightened but that everything was happening faster.

Scanning the open market, he took in the full picture of his surroundings, seeing the weavers, carpenters, smithies, wig makers and clocksmith bustling with the morning rush.

"It must have been overwhelming for Clovis, the offen, to take it all in. It would be like following the wind. Seeing the scenery through the eyes of an artist, no detail would be too small, but quite beautiful and revealing."

At the tallest church spires, he could see and hear the doves cooing, then the birds chirping in the courtyard bushes. But what stopped him was something behind all the movement of the market.

Settled under a fish cart, a small person was cowering behind the wheels. An instant magnetism caught them in their exchange of glances. Then in the baskets of the Hunalt tapestries, he saw another one, almost invisible, behaving like a scout in a plot to thieve.

"Could these be offens? Copernicus said they lived in ancient castles, lairs under bridges, or even a soddy built into the side of a hill. They are tiny, camouflaged miniature gypsies."

Within minutes, three of the small people were huddled under the fish cart, leering at Gaeten. Although their agility and deftness were outstanding, their faces were not young, but rather wizened like old, angry men, with their eyes burrowing into his.

Conferring among themselves and pointing at the livery boy, their voices carried to him like boomerangs.

"He sees the truth, so he must be sent by the seers. If he is a spy, what shall we do? Perhaps he was sent to betray us."

The youngest offen decided to take charge. "It is no longer good to run and hide and show our fear. We should seize the horseboy and find out if danger lies in wait for us."

Gaeten was stunned when the words of their whispers spoke loudly in his ears, with the vibration and resonance unfamiliar.

He quickly reached a conclusion in his own debate. "They are deep in their discussion and a bit frightened. I'll use that to my benefit and escape this standoff."

A flower and matchstick girl was about to pass with her basket, and at the moment she divided the space between Gaeten and the fish cart, he sprang into action. In a whirr, he jumped and spiraled into the hayloft over the livery and peered back through slatted boards at the confused trio.

"I must remember the seers' exact words. My senses will protect me. How do I avoid these little men? They plot to kidnap me, yet I had done nothing to rile revenge."

His breathing became rapid and he heard his own heart pounding. Reflecting back, he recalled Leonardo's sketches of Clovis and Punket and was startled by the similarities to these foreigners at hand. Oddly, others from the town passed, not noticing the tiny, conniving intruders or the magical disappearance of captivating, shiny objects.

"They certainly look ancient. I need to seek another door urgently . . . walls and bridges will be most likely. When my chores are done, I'll go to the cathedral and to the bridge by the Estuary."

Staying out of sight, Gaeten did his work at the livery. But his mind was occupied, planning his excursion in the darkness after the sun would go down.

The church bells rang out, louder than the bells he knew, and the veil of fog and the weight of the dew carried to him the music Puccini that would mimick in his operas.

"Leonardo spoke of the magic of Puccini, that the sense of sound is more acute when one closes the eyes." He sealed out the distracting sights and listened to the angelic aura.

Time had passed without warning when Gaeten realized darkness had descended. On the street and in the bushes, he no longer saw any sign of the offens.

7

Escape from the Offens

The flute-sized slide telescope from Galileo was focused on the stars before he lowered its scope to the cathedral's bell towers. Scanning each nook and cranny, he searched for signs of an offen. He reached into his pocket.

"I left the nautilus at Limoilou. I need it now, and Galileo will not be pleased I have forsaken his gift."

Above the parapet of the tower was an attic window sill, wide with open dormers. Perched on the edge was the dark shadow of an offen, dressed in a black oilcloth waistcoat with canvas britches. Gaeten noted his shortened legs and distinctive elfish shoes.

"Whatever he can do, I can do better," he mused quietly. "The masters didn't warn me of this or advise me of what threats I might face. Why do the offens care what I do?"

Gathering wood and cloth to soak in animal fat for a lantern, he lit it with a flint, knowing the moonlight would guide his feet.

The central courtyard was alive with night mongers and drunken seamen who paid no notice to the livery boy. A comforting sight and sound pierced the night as villagers lit their evening lamps.

Nearing the cathedral, he searched for a doorknob to appear in the walls and around the stone fencing.

Breaking through a bracket of bushes, he whispered, "Galileo, Copernicus, Leonardo!" Repeating it three more times, his confidence waned before his concentration was broken by a disruption in his surroundings.

Swinging around, he searched. He could smell an offen in the air and hear his eccentric humming jargon.

An offen was not all that he found, as the culprit also had Julien, holding him firmly by the ear. His brother's frightened eyes loomed from the shadows.

For an instant, Gaeten thought of his mother and the burden to keep Julien safe. He couldn't bear the thought of him coming to harm.

Taking three steps forward into the moonlight, Gaeten raised his hand with the invitation to negotiate a truce. The two squared off, both with eyes glaring to intimidate.

"Bonjours, mon ami. Je m'appelle Gaeten. I come in peace, but what cause do you have to take my brother from his home?"

A growly, deep voice emoted from a dwarf body of inestimable age. He had a distinctive mass of curly hair and few strands of silvery grey unkempt beard.

"The masters have sent you and it is fair that I have something to bargain with."

"Gaeten, help me," Julien pleaded, his blue eyes desperate and his freckled face tear-stained. "He said his people will eat me."

"What is your name, Sir?"

The offen stammered, "I am of Norman ancestry and herald from the monarchy of the world. We have been displaced throughout Europe only because of our appearance. You may call me Ruskin . . . I am the brother of Punket and the defender of my people. Your ancient seers exiled me and my friends for no fault of our own."

"What business do you have with me and my brother? We have done no harm to any offen. Why do you wish us ill will?"

"Do you deny that you are an agent for the masters of the brotherhood?"

Ruskin still had a firm grip on Julien but he shoved the lad forward a few steps into the moonlight.

"Are we not all agents of the Book of Knowledge? The world is an open door of opportunity for everyone. What do you fear?"

"My brother, Punket, was chased from the tunnels with Clovis, our disparaged leader. He had earned his spot in the brotherhood, then was denied an opportunity to defend his true character. Do you know of this?"

"Perhaps you can tell me your story, and I will better understand. But my brother has no cause here. He knows nothing of offens and you are his first sighting. Don't leave him with a fearful impression. Release him."

Ruskin took a sigh. "We have a camp down by the bridge. You and your brother come to meet my people— we live like gypsies because our rightful homes are denied. Saint-Malo has been our land for more than eight hundred years and we have pride in our contributions. We were once persecuted and forced out of Egypt, but none in Saint-Malo care about our noble heritage. Our tribal elders will want their opinions heard. Come now."

Julien was shoved forward until Gaeten could grasp his shirt to steady his feet.

In the moonlight, Gaeten and Julien followed Ruskin, and two others shuffled in behind on their heels.

The band of misfits tromped through a muddy marsh toward the river using reed torches sparingly, with Ruskin in the lead. The briar along the trail scratched their arms and faces, but it was the spring invaders of gnats and skeetos that caused the most aggravation.

Gaeten's senses were vigilant to the sounds of the meadow that was consuming him, hearing crickets singing, frogs croaking, garters and milk snakes slithering, and rodents grunting. He stopped to hear the choir of bluebells, then the fragrant lavender and the forget-me-nots chattering about nature's abundant favors.

"Can you hear it, Julien?"

"I hear a bunch of buzzing, that's all," Julien groaned, with his arms swatting at night insects.

"No, it's much more. It's the sound of life breathing and the world exhaling. You must listen to the music of your heart."

Through the reeds, Gaeten saw the glow of a campfire, surrounded by crude tents and decrepit oak wagons. The babble of a foreign language ceased when the new arrivals emerged.

The group of offens included all ages of the little men and women, and spry youngsters playing chasing games. A campfire crackled its welcome, with the spit roasting a feast of hare and brook trout.

Gaeten remembered his hunger at once, but decided to satisfy his stomach rumblings by taking in the constellations and feasting on the sounds that awakened all his senses.

Once more he wished he'd brought the nautilus.

An old woman ran at Ruskin with her arms flailing and a dialect no human would know.

"Glamiah, questo des sketchum pourqoi?"

Ruskin barked back something, that was equally undistinguishable to Gaeten. Julien moved tightly against his brother at the exchange.

The woman came closer to make her own inspection. "Blue eyes and hair the color of the sun—they are from Saint-Malo."

Gaeten could smell on her the sweet scent of wild lavender, then her breath and the reek of liquor as she peered inches from his nose. When their eyes locked, he was shocked to detect a wise soul with compassion and eons of seeing, and an earnest sense of motherhood.

Gaeten was compelled to ask, "Did you know my mother?"

The aged grandmother gazed for a long while.

"Yes, she came here once looking for wild herbs; she had a gentle heart but a weak body from malnourishment. Dear boy, you have her eyes and an adventurous soul."

Then a sadness flooded her face and she turned away.

"Please tell me more."

"I cannot give my strength to answer your questions. You are from the brotherhood."

Gaeten had a strong urge to turn and look behind, hoping a seer would be there to guide him. When he did, he saw the black silhouette of Saint-Malo rising above the fortress walls against the moonlight. The ancient castle turrets and Limoilou were sitting high over the sea, reaching out to him.

He strained his eyes to focus—the distant glow of a lantern at Limoilou narrowed its beam to the chimney on the mansard roof.

"Is it puffing a signal to me?"

Using a new enhanced vision, he could see that sitting on the peak of the roof were Copernicus, Galileo and another man that held a telescope.

A long board was teetering over the highest peak of the roofline. Galileo's arms were waving frantically as the other two balanced the board, then one at a time they climbed back to each end of the board letting their feet dangle in thin air.

He called upon his empowered talents to decipher their conversation by reading the lips of the three men.

"Good work, Socrates, we have proven the effects of gravity, polar balance and leverage!"

Gaeten wanted to laugh out loud, but Galileo was enunciating slowly, pointing to the stranger on the board.

Then Galileo waved a great Chinese paper kite. Gaeten knew it was a signal, recalling that Leonardo had once demonstrated a kite and later a parachute to a tunnel urchin, expounding that ancient kites were used to send rescue signals during wartime.

Da Vinci had an incredible inventor's mind, tuning to all things aero-mechanical. His fascination with bats and birds had become obsessive, studying their aerodynamics and wingspans, and on many days he was on the roof with pulleys and silk kites tied to his arms in anticipation of flight.

In Gaeten's desperate need for rescue, a telepathic message rang loud in Gaeten's thoughts. He listened.

"My friend Magellan will come for you, to the east footing of the bridge. A great brown owl will be on guard."

Gaeten gave a half-salute in acknowledgment, and minutes later the wave of a lantern replied.

Ruskin's head whipped around. "What are you staring at, horseboy?"

"So you know that I work at the livery. You have been watching me?"

Ruskin turned back to his tribe and didn't reply.

Instead, the offen people bound the two boys together by an itchy twine. In no time, the band of offens had gathered, becoming preoccupied in a discussion of what to do with the brothers, fearing they'd come for retaliation because of Clovis and Punket.

As their campfire burned down, some older ones broke away for a place to sleep and the children were sent to tents and wagons.

"Move over to the fire," Ruskin said. "Stay in the light of the flame so we can clearly watch both of you."

"Please, may we rest our feet in the water below the bridge," Gaeten said. "We're not used to rugged travel and have blisters from the stones and briar. I left my shoes in the courtyard. We will need to heal if you want us to travel tomorrow."

"Very well, but stay in my sight or you will be tied standing up for the rest of the night."

"Merci, Ruskin. It is kind of you."

Unbound and taking Julien's hand, Gaeten eased down the rocky slope to watch the shadows in the moonlight.

Almost an hour later, as the cool water was rippling around Gaeten's ankles, he poked Julien to ready himself.

"Ah, it is the wake of a small skiff."

The distinct calling of the great brown owl warned the boys of the approach of a dark fishing slew moving quietly. Inside, the man from the Limoilou roof was lying prone on his belly using a river pole to guide the raft.

"Are you Magellan . . . the great explorer, Ferdinand Magellan?" Gaeten whispered.

The gentle hoot of the owl and a loon's echo were signal enough to venture into the shallow creek. Magellan put his finger to his lips to caution silence.

Gaeten lifted Julien to the side and Magellan pulled him in, motioning to lie flat on the keel.

As the slew was about to drift out of sight around a bend, they saw offens with torches running toward them, then back and forth across the bridge, as they assumed the boys had escaped over the viaduct.

When it was safe to speak, Magellan raised himself to his elbows. He was an aged explorer with a round face, wired rim spectacles, and a full beard that covered half his face. As always, he wore a dark brown beret that sagged on his head.

"Gaeten, the intellects feared for your safety. As it happened, we were doing an experiment when Galileo heard your distress call. I have much to learn as well. How have you heard of me?"

"Cartier said that you sailed the ocean from the Pacific side by the Spice Islands to confirm Columbus's discovery that the world is round. Quite remarkable!"

"Under the Spanish flag no less," he laughed. "God bless my Portuguese mother. We were an army to be feared on the seas before we were called to battle. The Mactanese tribe off the coast of the Philippines fought long and fierce until I was overcome by their poison arrow. Although my body succumbed, my spirit and my memories remain with the brotherhood."

"It is valuable you have also come to preserve your great knowledge, with a heritage for future generations. Thank you for coming to rescue us. I remain always in your debt."

"The Book of Knowledge has no debt. We are comrades on the same mission. I will leave you at the harbor to find your way, and Galileo will see you soon."

"Travel well, then."

When Gaeten turned with a final adieu, the slew and Magellan had evaporated, and the water was smooth as if never disturbed. Looking up, the heavens sparkled with more diamonds than ever before in his memory, as a reassurance of peace.

Gaeten was up before dawn to complete his chores at the livery before collecting the morning catch and to mend lines with Monsieur Gallipeau.

The sunrise creeping over the horizon was fiery orange and iridescent pink, and he thought of Leonardo's knowledge of the depth of colors and its significance in the magnificent display of nature.

"This is the most beautiful time of day," he said. "I have faith that I have not denied the nautilus its beauty by hiding her. But I must allow the amulet to accompany me as she was meant to."

He poked the sleepy Julien. "Dear brother, it is time for you to grow up and help with the livery. You must finish the haying today."

Handing him the pitchfork, Gaeten gathered his fishing basket and left for his trading at the seashore. Skipping along the towpath, he halted at a movement in the tall grass.

"If it is another offen, I'll need to fend for myself. I don't have time for more distractions. I'll continue on . . . I'm a mariner's apprentice."

Clicking his heels in contentment, he jogged to the rocky slope to see his fishermen friends. It was a good day for selling his wares. The sun was still warm on his shoulders when the clock tower rang out that it was supper time.

Monsieur Gallipeau kept his promise and paid the lad two coins for his labors with the nets. He promptly left for the scribe's place of business.

"I shall buy some learning paper and a feather pen with a bottle of ink for my schooling with Monsieur Cartier."

At the scribe's shop, he settled on precise writing tools from his meager earnings, and in a canvas sack, he stored his tools. He slung the bag over his shoulder and headed up the hill facing Limoilou.

8

The Apprenticeship

It was early May, the time when the wildflowers were blooming in the pastures and the birds perched on the budding branches, singing with joy.

The old town stood solemnly around the great cathedral of Saint-Vincent-de-Saragoose, once a Benedictine Abbey in the 12th century. Its stained glass ceilings and windows were masterpieces of art, depicting the glory of Jesus and his disciples.

Gaeten knew many of the stories by heart, as told nightly by his mother before her death. Even now he could hear her angelic voice singing the revered hymns and psalms.

As a small boy, Gaeten had learned to whistle from the men frequenting the taverns. He knew the signal to summon help; it was from an ancient Greek language used to communicate between warriors.

As he hopped along the road, foraging and skipping stones, his breathing quickened on the rise to the manor house. He stopped to chew on a stem of purple lavender and catch a breath.

Emmanuel, in the yard giving the horses their oats, turned to wave to him.

"Bonjours!" Gaeten called. "It's a fine day."

Emmanuel sputtered a laugh. "What makes your day so fine?"

Gaeten became aware that he was carrying a bouquet of cowslips, hogweed, and lavender for Madame, and moved the posy behind his back.

"I have come to begin my apprenticeship with Monsieur Cartier. I will study his charts and maps and understand how to be a true mariner."

He followed the farmhand with his slop pail, and together they cornered a mother sow.

"Can't say that I'm not jealous," Emanuel said. "But I prefer to keep my two feet on solid ground that doesn't depend on the rising and falling of the ocean. I heard that Monsieur Verrazano was murdered by cannibals off the Carolinas."

"A gruesome story for sure, but we all get called to battle for the king at some time and place. It is our duty to die for a grand cause when that time has come. Did you not take up arms and defend France in the Italian Wars?"

"Oui, I did, and I'll follow the troops with a musket if I must. Now, is Madame expecting you?"

"I'm not sure that she does. Is that a problem?" Gaeten asked, wondering if he had been rude.

"This time of day, she'll be in her kitchen. Go around the back and knock."

Emmanuel looked at the bouquet and shrugged.

Partway up the lane, Gaeten stopped. "Emmanuel, do you ever hear strange sounds at night or see peculiar folks visiting the house?"

"I have only been inside the house once and nothing was unusual."

"Merci, Emmanuel, and thank you for covering my chores. I can come earlier tomorrow and help you with yours."

Madame Cartier was shaking the dust from a rug and hitting it with a wire fan when Gaeten rounded the corner. Setting her work aside, she wiped her hands on her apron. Her eyes lit up to see him.

"Bonjours, Gaeten, it is good to see you looking so well."

"I am back to my daily chores and business."

Awkwardly, he thrust the flowers in her direction, then dug into his basket and drew out a pouch filled with clams.

"I brought you enough fresh clams for a fine chowder."

"How thoughtful. I'll ask our cook to prepare one . . . you are here to see Monsieur Cartier, that is correct?"

"Yes, Madame, if that is suitable."

Her face showed her pleasure and she reached for the bouquet and the pouch. "Here, will you finish batting my rug while I take these to cool water."

While toiling with the rug, he heard an unfamiliar humming sound. A chill wind suddenly picked up and rushed through the back row of trees. As it grew louder, he wondered if his overactive senses were to blame.

"Have the offens followed me here?"

Just then, Madame returned. "Go on in through the kitchen, Gaeten. Monsieur is in his library waiting for you. Leave your boots outside the door and wash up at the basin."

At her words, he looked down, appalled at his own soiled appearance. His clothes were rarely washed and his dirty toes protruded from a leather sole that was held to his foot with tattered harness laces.

"It's no wonder the offens called me horseboy!"

Scrubbing with lye soap and water did little good, and his regretful appearance on his first meeting with Cartier dug into his confidence.

Cartier was preoccupied with his charts and barely looked up, but he was pleased to see his protégé had come for his first lesson.

"Bonjours, Monsieur Mansart. If you will agree, I'll refer to you simply as Gaeten, my apprentice in future."

"Oui, Monsieur Cartier. I brought my own journal and writing supplies to record every detail for study and comparison."

Cartier studied the disheveled lad and beamed at what he saw.

"Yes, I see you are ready, Gaeten. Sit here by the map desk. I have obtained the voyage journals of Verrazano's trip to New York island and Cape Fear five years ago. I understand that you have not been schooled in cursive writing, however, do your best and read through his notes then mark his route on this map and we will review your work together.

"Madame is excellent in penmanship, and we'll persuade her to give you a few lessons. She will enjoy that."

Gaeten's face showed elation that he might receive lessons from the lovely Catherine. He wondered if perhaps his mother would have been like her.

Cartier's booming laugh filled the room as his enormous presence turned to face Gaeten.

"I am an amiable, old mariner and will not bite you in spite of what you may have heard from Telesphore."

"And the atlases and diagonal, may I use those as well, Sir?"

"Indeed, consider this room your schoolhouse and I am your mentor. Seek out your answers however you choose, but always know that you have an answer. It was unfortunate that on our last voyage, Verrazano was eager for success and overlooked an obstacle that cost him his life. When you find the fatal error, we will celebrate."

Gaeten strode over to a wooden abacus standing on four legs beside the terrace window, daring not to touch it unless granted permission.

"Yes, that abacus will be helpful. For study purposes, let me propose that using Verrazano's last voyage, you calculate the required crew and days at sea. Count out the wine and biscuits needed to feed them, two per day, for the journey. Later we will take into account the salted meats and peas. That's a good starter to see how your skills adapt."

"I assure you, Monsieur, that I learn quickly from watching merchants in the market and I have an excellent memory for details."

The abacus rack, an ancient Arabic calculating system, contained a variety of rods, with sliding wooden beads that count between one and ten. Each bead slid to another position assumes a new value.

At first, Gaeten longed for a master to guide him with the tool, then it struck him that his senses have the power to do it on his own. Closing his eyes, he brought back a memory of Monsieur Hunalt using his abacus at the market.

"One goes here for a one-half franc and I'll pretend that a half franc is a crewman." His fingers slid the first wooden bead to the right side. "The journal claims a crew of 118 men when they set out, but only 93 returned after exploring the rocky shores of Newfoundland, then to Manhattan and to the West Indies at Guadeloupe.

"The short arrow marks in the Atlantic mean a strong current that makes progress slower, and the rock symbols warn of uncertain waters off the cod banks.

"Ah, oui, those barren slopes, I am inclined to believe that they are the land God gave to Cain. Impossible."

Within the hour, Jacques enquired of his progress and watched with care and amusement.

"Oui, Monsieur, I apologize for being slow, but my father told me as a boy that it's better to be late and accurate than speed through a project that fails. Soon my pace will improve."

"Ah, your father was a wise man then. Where is he?"

Gaeten regretted mentioning his father, who he had barely known, and especially building him up as a man of honor.

"He was tempted to seek his fortune in the East Indies and we never saw him again. Julien was very young and our mother had died, so we've been our own family."

Cartier toyed with his fingers, entertaining some thought. Examining the lad, he wondered how such a slight, impoverished boy had such immense spirit. The boy's hands and feet were calloused, and his skin was sunburnt and dirty, but underneath was something intriguing.

"Madame and I were not blessed to have children, but if I had a son, Gaeten, I would want him to be just like you. Always remember the wisdom of your father—slow and steady wins the race."

"Oh, it wasn't a race, just a carpentry job."

Monsieur broke into laughter, then walked over and tousled Gaeten's blond curls.

"My instincts in choosing you were absolutely correct! It is getting much too dark to work by the light of a lantern. Go home now to your brother and come tomorrow before supper, and we will get more done."

Cartier himself longed for the boy's return. Catherine was waiting in the hallway outside the library when Gaeten opened the door.

"Bonsoir, Madame Cartier."

"I've been waiting to talk to you, Gaeten. I heard some talk last night of you being rescued from the offen camp. You and your brother must have been terribly frightened. Myself, I've never met an offen but I know they are different sorts and some are prone to nastiness."

"It's very kind of you to be concerned, Madame, but I am most grateful that Galileo heard my plea for guidance. The masters gave me a special gift of heightened senses. I knew that I was capable of getting us out of the situation. The offens are more confused than harmful."

Excitement rose in his voice, re-enacting his memories. "Did you know that Ferdinand Magellan came for me on a raft?"

Catherine's eyes were wide with the imagination of the sight of the elders. She remembered the days when she lived at the des Granche manor and how her father told her fascinating stories of his noble adventures with the king.

"Then it proves you are a special boy for Magellan to be sent for the rescue. You do understand that you didn't come here by accident." The preposterous idea intrigued him but he didn't want Catherine to see his failings.

"Galileo flew a kite as a message. I knew that meant someone was coming to help us get away."

Catherine crossed her arms and cupped her hand to cover her lips as she tried her best not to smile.

"I will come again tomorrow. The Monsieur asked me to come before supper."

"Then I will make a special dessert if you will be our honored guest."

The two stood with a knowing glance, aware their friendship and understanding would last forever.

"Tomorrow, before you leave, the masters would like you to visit. I've arranged for you to go up to the spare room near the attic. They will wait for you."

In the late hours, the town square was quiet. Gaeten was not tired but was exhilarated. Only the laughter emanating from the tavern and a lone lamplighter on the street were the signs of life.

He looked up to check out the young boy on stilts lighting the street lanterns. "Bonsoir, what is your name?"

"I am Louis. I have seen you working at the livery, but no one pays heed to me. You are Gaeten."

"I'm sure you see a lot from up there. Do you ever see offens come out at night . . . you know, the little people?"

Looking both ways first, Louis answered.

"Shh, don't speak of them or they will hear you. Perhaps sometime I will come to the livery and we'll talk, Gaeten."

Louis moved away from the lantern's light, frightened that an offen might appear out of the darkness.

The next day went quickly and Gaeten could hardly wait to get to Limoilou. The uphill climb took little energy as he bounded with his seafood basket to the back kitchen.

Catherine was bringing in freshly baked bread from the outer clay oven. He followed her as she laid the wooden boards out for the bread to cool. Crossing her arms at her waist, she took a step back to face Gaeten.

"My dear boy, I hope you will not be insulted but I have requested a bath be prepared for you outside the garden door. Today will be special and you will want to scrub off the stable soil."

Catherine handed him a bar of soap and a drying rag and gestured that he get on with it.

"Certainement, Madame!"

Shirking his soiled clothing, Gaeten eased into the wooden barrel already filled with suds. It was a wondrous feeling, like swimming in the hole on Normandy hill after a hot day. A short time later he stood at the kitchen door waiting for Madame's inspection.

"Bonjours, Gaeten, come in. We will sup before Monsieur gives you today's lesson."

"I have never supped with anyone before, Madame, and I apologize that I don't know my manners."

"Always hold the door open for your elders, be respectful to everyone, and most important is to wait for the lady of the house to be seated before you dig in." She laughed. "After Monsieur gives a thankful prayer for our food, you may eat what is on your plate—oh, and try to keep your elbows off the table."

"I will do my best."

"My father, Monsieur des Granches, will be joining us. He likes to tell stories, so be kind and listen. You can always learn something from your elders."

"Of course, Madame."

Catherine held an ivory linen funeral shirt that she recovered and prepared for Gaeten.

"I found this lovely shirt and a pair of britches in the attic that will fit you quite well. They are washed and pressed. I left a comb on the washstand also, and if you need help, call me."

"Merci, merci. You are too kind, Madame."

His face flushed with the awkwardness of the situation as he became aware of his beleaguered condition.

The dinner progressed around a long dining table with Monsieur and Madame Cartier at each end and Gaeten seated across from Jacques des Granches. The aged gentleman walked with a slight stoop and a walking stick, but he was alert as a jackrabbit. The constable studied Gaeten, making assessments of the boy's fortitude.

Catherine's siblings had blessed him with grandchildren, that he was mentoring in the skills of the bourgeois. His hope was that one day his family would again be represented in the king's court.

Gaeten waited for Catherine to take her seat, and as she rang a bell at the table, a woman in crisp, white aprons entered carrying platters and casseroles, the like that he'd never seen before.

In fear of his lack of etiquette, he watched and waited as the woman rounded the table, finally arriving at his side with a quail on a platter surrounded by root vegetables. With two large spoons together like shovels, she filled his plate with generous portions. He watched how Madame used her utensils and did his best to mimic her.

Des Granches said, "Gaeten, my dear boy, Catherine tells me you are training to be a mariner. You realize that first the commission must be proposed before the Abbott, then the king. Will you be ready when the orders come through?"

"I am working my hardest, and it would be an honor to voyage with Monsieur Cartier. Sometimes he looks at me through his monacle to read my understanding and I try not to disappoint. We agreed that our motto is slow and steady."

With an after-thought, des Granches turned to Catherine. "The Abbott, his Lordship le Veneur, has inquired if he should expect a dinner invitation shortly. You will need to plead your case with him as the king will not hear of your application without the Abbott's approval. I assured him I would make an inquiry on his behalf."

"I have investigated about ships that might come available in the spring," Cartier said. "It could be either next year or the one after. The king's fleet is becoming ancient and I would like assurances of a seaworthy vessel or two."

"You returned on Verrazano's Seraphine and the Dauphine did you not?"

"Oui, dear father, but Girolamo hopes to continue his brother's quest to the Carolinas. It has been proven that gold and silver are easily gained in the Gulf of México. But I do not seek my fortune in precious cargo, rather I hunger to follow the great Seaway, and to stake the fleur-de-lis and establish French settlements. The more settlements, the more villages, the more traders, and the more pelts for the French economy."

"That is indeed a noble quest and would appeal to King Francis. He remains hopeful that the passage to Cathay and the riches beyond are yet to be discovered. I have news that Cabot, the Basques, and Normans have also found a great fishing harvest on the banks of the New Found Land."

Gaeten hung onto every word with awe, enthralled at the intelligence of these great men. Catherine caught a glance and gestured that he should not forget to eat his dinner. He only spoke when asked a question and waited for a cue from Catherine to be excused from the table.

Cartier nodded to the boy.

"Come, Gaeten, the men will adjourn to the library and enjoy one of my fine brandies. All mariners find refuge in the spirits, especially after days of gales and storms on the sea."

With a wink, Catherine closed the library doors and departed to the parlor for some needlework and repairs.

"Father des Granches, Gaeten will accompany my first voyage in the crow's nest. I will depend on him for his sights on the horizon and the checking of our nautical measurements and calculations."

Cartier smiled proudly at his new protégé.

"Perhaps you would like to show Monsieur des Granches the route we plan to take."

Jacques had moved to the great table where the charts lay exposed and now small objects were exactly positioned. One such item was a brass miniature of a sailing ship.

"Oui, Monsieur, it is reasonable that we use Verrazaano's routing when he discovered New York and the Isle of Manhattan, however, we will turn at the sight of the great fishing banks and follow the Seaway.

"I am studying the cartography and navigation journals of previous explorers like Cabot and Magellan to borrow their excellent knowledge. But most of all, the guiding light is in the celestial heavens, as we can never be lost as long as Polaris is there. I have studied Galileo's theories and analysis of measurements."

Gaeten was bursting inside, biting his lip not to expose his attic friends.

"Indeed, young man, it is wise to learn from the experience of others and not repeat their mistakes. Show me on the map, the route Monsieur Cartier will follow."

Gaeten's hand shook slightly as he pointed along a line installed on a map by Cartier. Monsieur des Granches was leaning close to his shoulder, intent on his moves.

"It is best to leave Saint-Malo in the spring, perhaps April or May when the seas are calm. It is impossible to predict when a tempest or gale will interfere with our schedule, but we have allowed for that in our calculation of supplies. That would give the crew the summer months to travel along the rivers and make settlements. Monsieur Cartier has suggested we need a fleet of three manned ships."

Gaeten's voice cracked with nervousness. He looked up at Cartier and saw the delight in his face.

Granches nodded his approval. "I see, Jacques, that you have found yourself your first crewman. Show me more."

Cartier read out excerpts from other explorers' journals, then cited their experiences with native tribes.

"The Jesuits have been attempting to convert Hurons and Iroquois to Christianity. Some have been successful while others have given their lives without avail. We know the tribes of Micmacs and Iroquois will trade pelts and skins to build alliances."

"Oui, Jacques, but the natives will comprehend the land as no Frenchman has. A resource with reward is not to be feared, they can offer a pathway to what you seek. The Spanish can plunder the gold and silver of Brazil and the Carolinas, while you choose to seek fortunes in trade in this new world—riches of another value—the king's coffers. The Italian wars have depleted the king's economy."

"I agree. My hope is to find a saqamaw, an advisor from the tribe, as a guide and translator from the habitation. Some native groups are hostile, but others freely offer friendship."

Des Granches lingered over the charts and maps and continued to pepper Cartier with questions and concerns.

"Jacques, it is late and my carriage will be here shortly. I am impressed with your preliminary proposal. May I suggest that we invite the Abbott in say—two weeks?"

Cartier darted a glance at Gaeten. "Yes, it will be great labor, but we will be ready. Refer your request to Catherine as she sees you out."

"It has been a pleasure."

He shook hands with Cartier then moved toward Gaeten. "And also to meet you, Monsieur Gaeten. Do you have a last name?"

"We have been Mansarts since birth, but few people know my father's name."

"I will hold Gaeten Mansart in high regard," Des Granches announced.

9

Rendez-vous with the Masters

Gaeten bounded up the great stairway to the room near the attic. His heart pounded with anticipation to see Galileo, Copernicus, da Vinci, and Magellan.

A freshly laundered, mended and pressed shirt hung on the back of a chair, similar to one he'd worn on his arrival.

"Suffering saints, that's mine. Madame is too kind." Leaving the linen funeral shirt in exchange, he stood before a plain plastered wall.

"Bonjour, mon amis, I have come for our conference."

The wall grew fuzzy until a door slowly appeared, then a glowing brass knob.

He turned the handle to gain entry.

The distinguished group of eager faces waited to hear of his encounters with the offens and about his escape, knowing yet inquiring.

"I am glad to see you all again. I must thank you for giving me the gift of my senses. Knowing that I had my own abilities to get out of a tough situation made me stronger in head and body."

Copernicus said, "You must never underestimate the gifts you were born with. But please tell us of your adventure with the offens. We didn't expect such an early encounter or we would have given you a better direction."

The sage looked deep into Gaeten's soul. "And the powerful nautilus, did it guide you?"

The lad's look of shame was his only reply to Copernicus.

"I was grateful for Galileo and Magellan being on the roof and signaling to us. I believe the offens were harmless but I couldn't take chances with Julien. The first one was Ruskin, the ringleader, and brother of Punket. He was agitated but protested that his brother had been misunderstood in his pranks with Clovis. I thought it best to hear him out."

"A good decision, but when I heard you call for Galileo, we knew you needed help," da Vinci said. "Fortunately, Magellan had joined us, and as an explorer, he would be the best rescue. Ferdinand insisted he knew the river and the bridge where you were."

"Thank you, Monsieur Magellan, for coming down the river. We were relieved to see your shadow in the moonlight. It was a brave undertaking. Also, I would like to hear about the experiment on the roof that night."

Magellan and Galileo laughed about that.

"Idle minds make no progress," da Vinci said. "While watching the celestial movements and studying the constellations from the rooftop, we decided to test our weights versus gravity and the equalizing balance to create leverage."

"It gave us new clarity in understanding gravity," Galileo said, "which is the pull of the moon and the controller of tides. We documented the event so that others may learn."

He guffawed as they snickered. "We confess we almost lost our friend over the roof in a slight miscalculation."

"Indeed," Magellan recounted. "It was thrilling to be hanging over the edge of the sea on a board. As a child I once swung off the mast of a ship into the briny drink. It was invigorating, but now that I am older, I have the disadvantage of fear. My colleagues were convincing though and I quite enjoyed the experiment."

"Leonardo had been perfecting the Chinese kite and wanted to test it out," Copernicus said. "Although there is a considerable calculation of the wind and distances, it is an experiment nonetheless."

"Tell us more about your experience with the dwarves— the offens at their village," Galileo interjected.

"They are much in the likeness of Leonardo's drawings and have outstanding agility in their hands and feet. They are no taller than me, dwarfish and gypsy-looking, ancient with withered faces. The men have long straggly beards."

"Were you mesmerized by their eyes?"

"When Ruskin looked into my eyes, I did feel a magnetism, that my soul could betray me."

Behind the masters, Gaeten saw the images of other unknown inventors, one controlling the force of air in a concoction called the bellows. The forced air was sent to a gear that puffed and groaned to start the up and down motion of a chugging lever.

Gaeten looked around the room's fascinating course of events with curiosity and without query.

"When do I get to learn from the masters?" he asked.

Copernicus said, "First, we ask that you go through the crevice and retrieve the parchments that Clovis stole."

"Is it safe?"

"The spring runoff from the rains has not yet entered the tunnels. The route is rugged and you must be deft with your feet. When the water rises, it is muddy and difficult. Leonardo has drawn a map of your path. You'll need better shoes for climbing . . . those won't do at all."

Gaeten removed the pieces of flat leather tied with laces around his ankles. Copernicus returned seconds later with well-cobbled, dusty shoes, bigger than Gaeten's feet but with long, leather laces around the boot. The seer rubbed his chin while reminiscing.

"I met an Italian cobbler named Geppetto," Copernicus said. "He insisted that I take these for a well-deserving lad such as you." He sniggered at his memory.

Sliding his soiled feet into the shoes, Gaeten felt a euphoria of new comfort.

"I have never had real shoes before. Merci, Copernicus. The Italian is a fine cobbler indeed."

He lifted his knees high in a few steps, then clomped the shoes on the ground. "I must appear like a prancing horse." He burst in laughter and the men joined in.

"You will adjust soon to the weight. They are yours to keep. They've been here for over fifty years but still have plenty of wear and a few tales to go with the eons."

Leonardo opened a scrolled map on two handles, and his boney index finger followed the route. "Take some of my paints to mark the walls so future travelers will find their way without hazard."

"Here and there will be a ledge to rest. Your journey will take less than an hour and we'll watch from the crevice with instruction. Carry this sack with lantern oil and torches."

Magellan asked his friends, "It is almost midnight, should he still go tonight?" All the faces turned to Gaeten.

"I am eager to help, so the sooner the better."

"An odd thing to say, but yes, I agree," Galileo said.

Slinging the sack of supplies over his shoulder, he followed his comrades to the crevice. Galileo gave him the lantern and shook his hand like a king sending a warrior into battle.

Gaeten bowed and saluted, accepting the great honor, then took his first step into the cavern. In the darkness, the lantern cast long shadows.

Wriggling and squeezing, he made it through the first section without difficulty. Looking back, it was humorous to him to see four faces peering in with all their hopes placed on him.

"It is all good," Gaeten called back. His voice rang in an echo through the first chamber, and the four elders laughed at its musical sound.

For the first time, he reached into his pocket and felt the warm, magical talisman. In the darkness, it glowed an iridescent beauty that filtered out through the fabric of his clothes.

Continuing on the rocky ledge, he came to a second tight spot that required more upward agility. He held onto the wall for stability and found water trickling onto his hands. Setting the lantern up high, he pulled his lithe body up on the edge.

Overhead, a primate Ichthyornis seabird flapped its wings and cried a cawing sound through the cavern. Gaeten knew the dinosaur-bird would have a razor-sharp bite.

In the distance, the four elders peered their approvals, and a whisper swirled toward him in the tunnel.

"Don't worry, Gaeten, Ickty is following like a faithful pet. If anything attacks, he'll swoop in to defend you. He's a lonely orphan needing a friend. Make him feel welcome."

"I am well-supervised then." With a laugh, he raised his hand for the red peaked dinosaur-bird to show submission. Its long neck began to writhe and squirm, and with humility, its great talons took long strides toward him.

But a sudden nest of water snakes circled Gaeten, and his agile feet recoiled out of their reach. He waved the lantern low for the fire to repel the serpents, then waved it overhead at a camp of bats on the upper rocks.

"Aha, that's the height of the ceiling."

As the torch shone onto the entrance to the next tunnel, he stepped inside to search for signs of the stolen journals. Squinting, he focused on Ickty, who was advancing slowly with a gentle purring sound.

The medieval bird's scales flamed in fluorescent colors of purple and brilliant indigo. The intensity of its green and amber eyes softened to expose a gentle ancient soul, and as he approached, he gained the confidence to trust the adventurer.

Swish, swish, caw, caw!

Gaeten reached out his hand to encourage the dinosaur-bird to approach. "Here boy, good boy!"

He held still as Ickty smelled him and breathed into his nose and ears. The giant bird nuzzled against his leg and rested his head to ease his loneliness, then gave a satisfied heave.

They said Clovis planned to escape with the journals through the farthest entrance, but Galileo said that it would be sealed off and impossible for anyone to come and go.

Ickty grasped the telepathy of Gaeten's thoughts and replied with sounds of choking and gurgling.

Suddenly, a thunderous, deep roar from the tunnel echoed the word 'Thoth'. Gaeten covered his ears from the piercing pitch and opened his eyes to a burst of fire-spewing toward the journals from far into the tunnel.

"Easy boy, easy." His whisper was like the day with Catherine's stallion when he had stared the frightened horse in the eyes and breathed into its nostrils.

On tiptoes, he saw light beyond the crevice and surveyed the source of the fire burst. He knew he had traveled several miles and surmised that Galileo would calculate an exact distance.

"The only fire-breathing creatures I've heard of were in Greek mythology or Leviathan's ancient ancestors, but surely those are extinct. Copernicus described a prehistoric offspring, nesting in uninhabited caverns. Did he mean a fire-breathing dragon? Or was testing me, that the news might frighten me off. Of course, it wouldn't."

His thoughts echoed to be understood by Ickty, the dino-bird, and he raced to claim Gaeten's shoulder as a refuge to secure his adoption.

When Levi, the fire serpent-dragon, saw the pair together, he first cowered, then recovered and attempted to mimic Ickty.

Gaeten hid any fear and marveled at the beauty of the great serpent, Levi, with his gleaming green eyes, pearly blue scales, and orange and red transparent webbed wings. On his head was a horned knob, and his muscular serpent body was pulled along by its long, powerful neck.

With a final puff of flames, the serpent-dragon settled quietly, letting his breathing slow and his fire abate.

Although centuries older, Levi presumed that Ickty was of his own species and was ecstatic with the reunion. The chatter in a series of mutual groans signaled an agreement to friendship, and feeling secure, Ickty left Gaeten and moved over to lick the neck of the fire-serpent.

"Good boy, that's it, slow and steady. You are two of a kind, both longing for companionship," Gaeten whispered in a magical dinosaur language that came from his lips, but he'd never learned, with sounds that altered from the highest pitch to the lowest depth.

A truce of understanding gave them all security.

Gingerly, Gaeten and the two misfits followed the creek bed, stopping within a stretch of the stolen parchments. He squatted at a nest of straw, feathers, and cobwebs, that appeared to be the home of a minuscule, nocturnal creature.

Brushing droppings aside, he picked up a clay cylinder pipe lying on top of the book. The corner of a document was visible inside, but the light of the lantern was too dim, so he slid the pipe into his sack.

Taking stock, he gave grateful pats to his prehistoric allies, as it was time to go their own ways.

"Thank you, my new friends. I wish you could stay and tell me more about yourselves and where you have come from, so I could write a report for the sages. It is remarkable that our times in life have intersected here."

Leviathan hung his head in sadness at the separation, and Ickty cawed a farewell greeting that they understood.

"I have seen the wisdom of the ages and you will help create the future, Gaeten. We will meet again one day, sooner than you think."

The serpent dinosaur gave a deep sigh as if his heart were breaking, and Ickty was quick to console his new friend.

Gaeten watched as the pair hobbled away to retrace their route into the caverns. The distant cooing became fainter, with their sounds of splashing and frolicking in the creek.

Why would the great serpent leave with such a cryptic message?
A final bellow of sadness echoed to bid him adieu.

Leonardo had used a roll of fibered parchment paper from the Mediterranean to wrap and preserve the treasured scrolls. Staring at the papyrus, an aura of intrigue surrounded Gaeten and he felt an urgency to share it as soon as possible with the masters. With care, he packed the book and scrolls and tied secure straps around the corners.

I wonder if the scrolls have been touched by the spells of Thoth.

Engrossed in their mystery and awe, he lost track of time until shivers ran up his spine.

The nautilus . . . its radiance is bright enough to glow on the path.

Within a few feet, he stopped, sensing the presence of someone else. A warm breeze and an echo carried to him the humming by an offen campfire somewhere.

I'm not alone!

He whispered an ominous query to the sages. "Bonjours, my wise friends, do you hear this echo?"

The few seconds of silence seemed like eons before he heard a chorus of replies urging him toward the crevice.

He recognized da Vinci's voice, beckoning him. "Light will always guide you, Gaeten. Follow us like you would search the stars."

Halfway into the tunnel, he came to an archway and a rock-lined chamber, crusted with quartz and moss. With da Vinci's brush and paint, he dabbed a wall marking to prevent misdirection.

Stabilizing his weight against the wall, his fingers stubbed a sharp object, then his arm felt a trickle of blood. With the amulet for light, he searched for the source. The wall glistened with crystals and silver veins, but it was a great sword wedged in the rock that cut into his flesh.

"The Excalibur!" he shouted. "Surely it is another's sword. These mighty halls may hold the world's secrets and epiphanies. The elders will want to know more."

He tore a strip from his shirt to tie around the wound.

Further down the path, he slowed at the sound of water dripping, then stumbled over another artifact. He squatted to pick it up.

An ivory, carved drinking horn . . . definitely foreign to this cave.

"Perhaps the offens left this behind . . . Clovis or Punket." He froze. "Or if it's been stolen from the Book of Thoth, there'd be a curse to the person who touches it."

Gaeten's hands were red and hot, and he lowered the light to the path to examine a footprint with many toes.

"The footprint has many toes . . . like an offen. Clovis?"

Driven by curiosity, he glanced at the script's drawings, but the symbols and hieroglyphics were undecipherable. He jolted upright at a deafening howl from the cavern that started rocks and debris to tumble above his head. Grasping the relic, he dodged the falling boulders and fled to the far wall. The document was scorched at the edges and burst into flames and ashes at Gaeten's feet.

"What have I done? It couldn't be the dinosaurs, as they were long gone. Have I activated the spell of Thoth?"

Feeling along the jutted wall, he searched for the opening of the hidden chamber, past the glow over the shimmering ripples of the rivulet and water pools. The ceiling was a haven of crystallite, with spikes of frozen, pristine mineral particles draped in a magnificent formation, surrounding a tiny waterfall.

Bending beside the lake, he cooled his hands and listened. The distant echoes of the seers had faded.

"Galileo read to me of Aristotle's works about the analyses of objects and theories. A sight of this beauty cannot be cursed. Surely nature's abundance must be a good omen."

Taking refuge from the roar of the quake, he lingered to draw images on the back of the map document.

His eyes opened wider as a jagged shard fell from the ceiling, piercing the lake like the Excalibur, King Arthur's sword, used in the battle against Mordred three hundred years before.

"I'll remember this as a wondrous sight. I understand it better, and I see the value of recording the earth's enlightenment, secrets, and knowledge."

A nearby rustling flushed a wave of vulnerability over him. Reaching to his britches for the slingshot, he massaged the willow strapping and readied his aim with a handful of lake pebbles.

But his thoughts stopped him. "Hmmph . . . gravity and velocity."

He reflected back to Galileo's and Magellan's roof experiment. "They say Magellan resolved the circumference theory from the Atlantic to the Pacific. Ah, to be an explorer of the world."

He fired a pebble into the lake and watched the circles, then another. "Leonardo would see the beauty in this too, but so must have Clovis and Punket."

He shot more pebbles again and again into the lake, then stopped to listen to a whisper.

"Is that you, Gaeten?"

From the shadows, a creature appeared, with dirty, worn shoes with curled toes.

"Who goes there?" he called out.

Ruskin stepped out of the darkness. "I knew you would come for the book so I have waited."

The offen rubbed his bruised forehead and allowed the torchlight to shine on him.

"How did you get in here, Ruskin?"

"Would you tell all your secrets simply because you're asked? I could ask who came to your rescue at the bridge."

Gaeten continued, "Did the offens send you here or do you plan to steal the legends?"

Ruskin held his hands over his head in a gesture of surrender. "Why do you accuse me to be a thief?"

"You have not answered a single question of mine." Gaeten raised his voice to echo back through the crevice to be heard by the seers. "I insist that you tell me how you got into the tunnels."

Ruskin took a pause. "Clovis and Punket served your masters for centuries and learned the secrets of the caverns and tunnels like the backs of their hands. If I tell you how I got in, you will seal that access so I cannot return."

"That may be true, but why do you want to come here? The Book of Knowledge is not for barter but it is for the preservation of future worlds including the masters, our families . . . and yes, the offens too."

Ruskin smiled for the first time. "You are too trusting, Gaeten. The masters are afraid of the offens and don't trust us. But fear is its own enemy. We are a band of people without a homeland. We look different and speak a dialect you don't hear.

"Are you gypsies then?"

"We are called all sorts of species, from leprechauns, nymphs, dwarfs, gypsies and worst of all . . . goblins. We are proudly tradesmen, hunters, and craftsmen."

"Do you have powers?" Gaeten asked.

"If you call it a power, most of all we can camouflage ourselves and vanish."

"I'm confused. If the sages lived in harmony with offens for hundreds of years, what changed? What will convince the sages of your assurance not to interfere with their works or the collection? More than words of a promise, can you demonstrate your honesty? Why did you come here today?"

"I was waiting for you, to apologize for threatening you. We meant no harm. To most folks, we are almost invisible, but you stared back. I assumed you were under Thoth's spell. I was surprised that you saw me under the cart and I couldn't have you running back to the masters. They would find me and cast me out as a defector. That's no way to live when you look over your shoulder everywhere you go."

Gaeten nodded his understanding. "I was not around when the events took place with Clovis, so I have no judgment. They will not condemn you simply because you are Punket's brother. That would defy the principle quest of reason and knowledge, as all conclusions *must* be proven."

"Are you certain, Gaeten?"

"Yes. But tell me . . . I've been warned that excerpts of the documents carry a curse. Are you certain that *you* have not been plagued with it?"

Ruskin's face contorted. "I cannot answer when I do not know for sure."

A piece of pearly blue scale slipped from the offen's hand to the ground at Gaeten's feet.

"That belongs to Leviathan," Gaeten declared. "Where did you get it?"

"It was beside me when I woke up from a nap in the tunnel. I remember that someone came to comfort me, but my dreams will not return to explain it."

"Search your heart truth and be prepared to answer the sages. Come with me and we will return what was taken."

Ruskin stopped him. "First, you should know that when Clovis devised his scheme, I tried to oppose it."

"It's important to know that, my friend."

"There would be more advantages if the masters and the offens worked together, rather than be enemies."

"Come, Ruskin, follow me."

The two small people trudged through the creek and climbed the ledges until they were close to the crevice. Past the last turn, a beam of light silhouetted them.

The sages awaited the precious cargo that Gaeten carried with caution. Immediately, they became protective to the point of ordering a security contingent to seize the boys the instant they passed through the crevice.

Behind the four stepped a great man with a head of curls and chiseled face. His hands reached to take the revered, lost journals. Stepping aside, the others bowed for the man to begin the inquiry.

"Aristotle," Gaeten said, recognizing him at once. His jaw dropped to see the greatest thinker of all masters.

The man's unfamiliar voice resonated, and remaining stone-faced, he pointed his finger as a warning.

"Prepare, my friends, for an intruder and deception."

Aristotle, from ancient Greece, was a respected theorist on believability and character, a renowned philosopher and scientist from early biblical times. The ancient Greeks could make an astute judgment of a stranger's credibility and trust.

Gaeten sensed an extraordinary aura of honor surrounding Aristotle, and in awe, he watched a cloud of moving footprint tracks that followed the giant's steps.

"Take into account, gentlemen, that anybody can become angry and that is easy," Aristotle said. "But to be angry with the right persons, to the right degree, and the right time, for the right purpose, and in the right way. That is *not* within everybody's power and is *not* easy."

Gaeten whispered to Ruskin the identity of the Greek mythologist. "It's Aristotle, the leader of our thoughts. Take heed of his words and let them guide your mind."

Ruskin was overcome, in the presence of greatness, and bowed until Artistole took his elbow to set him upright.

"Bonjours, Messieurs, I am Ruskin, from the offens. I mean no harm and have come to make amends. It is an honor to meet the great thinkers of our past and present."

Ruskin stood humbled as he spoke. "Gaeten convinced me that you would listen to my motives with conciliatory hearts. I am the brother of Punket, but I did not agree with Clovis's scheme. Am I to be punished simply because of the blood that runs through my veins?"

His hands folded in front and his head bent to wait for acceptance from any sage.

Aristotle's head tilted as he examined Ruskin's plea, and considered his displayed sense, but said nothing. Leonardo withdrew to contemplate while Galileo and Copernicus joined together in hushed conversation.

Aristotle whispered for only the offen to hear. "Knowing yourself is the beginning of all wisdom. Remember this truth. I say, Monsieur Ruskin, that you will earn your due without condemnation."

10

Magic of the Great Rooms

Gaeten addressed the curious sages, gathered close to learn more. "Ruskin has apologized for kidnapping me. It was out of fear for his own safety, and he was glad I escaped on the river. But he can speak for himself."

"Come inside now, Ruskin," Copernicus said. "You understand we have many questions."

Ruskin led them into the inner sanctum, and removing a basket of acorns from a stump, he took a seat near Gaeten, who sat in a canvas sling hanging from a branch.

A hush of anticipation fell over the cavern as a scurry of shy raccoons, possums, hedgehogs, and a conglomeration of marsupials retreated into the foliage.

From the tree limbs, their peculiar faces listened to the masters, expelling nature's sounds of oohs and aahs, with whispers from the background. "He's an offen," said a voice from the woods. "I wonder if he's one of the bad ones that took part in the thieving of the journals. Perhaps he brings the spell of Thoth."

Compassion was in the eyes of Copernicus and da Vinci, but Galileo remained suspicious.

Aristotle continued his questioning of Ruskin's soul. "Monsieur Ruskin, I feel you have a reason to fear the curse of Thoth. Although we know that your brother interfered with a spell, have you?"

"Sir, I don't . . . "

"You cannot tell untruths here before the sages. We are all-seeing and all-knowing. We are immortal."

Ruskin stammered, "I . . . I do not know, Sir."

"You have something to say to us," Galileo pressured. "Answer Aristotle's question."

"I don't know about the spell. Clovis was cursed when he dove for the golden box in the river. Legend says it's punishment for touching the treasure, that serpents and scorpions would devour the flesh and the spirit would remain tormented for eternity. You see me as I stand here before you, I am of the flesh and have not been devoured.

"It was said that Clovis was driven madly to his death and Punket also died at only three hundred years. I have committed no crime to have such a punishment. Although I suffer the angst of my brother, I bear no guilt in the deception of the parchments. It was only today when Gaeten retrieved the journals that I was within touch of the excerpts."

Aristotle's face softened to understand. "As Clovis interfered with the scrolls, we know he received a curse. But you've presented your honesty and soul before us and that is good. There is no injustice in truth."

Ruskin bowed.

"Merci, my good sages. Monsieur Aristotle, you have given me comfort in my heart. And I remember you, Monsieur Galileo, from a past time here working on inventions, a time when we trusted each other before Clovis was infected."

"I remember, Ruskin. The times were precious."

"Our older offens tried to talk Clovis out of his plan and to convince Punket not to be a party to betrayal. But Clovis was determined and Punket thought he could deter him from his thievery."

Aristotle's hand rested on Ruskin's shoulder. "I must return now to my place in the forum at Athens. There I will reject Plato's theories and continue my quest of knowledge."

The philosopher raised his cloaks to leave and turned back with final wisdom. "Ruskin, seek beauty in all that is abstract."

As Aristotle strode out of sight, the ground was left reverberating from his footsteps. He reappeared on a statue with an ivory base in Athens, posing in thought to oversee the world and mankind.

With the shame of his confession of failure, Ruskin shriveled by a foot of height in front of their eyes.

Gaeten panicked. "What is happening, Ruskin? It can't be a spell!"

"Offens have unique characteristics. We diminish in size when we are fearful or with rejection, and we give ourselves away with a lie. It takes inner power to overcome."

"How can we be sure you are not under the curse?" Galileo challenged. "I haven't seen this in your ancestors. Is what you say truthful? Is truth not power?"

"Our community shares these senses. Today, in sympathy, others in my tribe will experience the same physical reduction. Do you recall what the offens contributed to the Book of Knowledge? Test me with a question for which I would know the answer. If I answer incorrectly, you will see me get bigger, the mark of shame belonging to a liar."

The sages put their heads together, then Galileo spoke.

"When Leonardo arrived, one of his early paintings here was of an offen. Who was it?"

Ruskin answered without a flinch.

"I recall Clovis sitting for a portrait for Monsieur da Vinci. He wore my grandfather's beret that my grandmother made for him. It was dark green like moss from the woods, rimmed with a sewn golden braid. You will see an angry look in the eyes of Clovis. If you have the picture, you can verify what I have said."

Da Vinci went to his art table to retrieve the drawing from his portfolio. Staring at the work, he was drawn to the depths of deception. The moment of the painting was impressed on his memory, as Clovis had betrayed himself with seething hatred, and he could not deny that in his eyes.

Leonardo returned to Ruskin. "The eye of the beholder cannot fib. The description you give is correct for Clovis. I recall he was impatient and kept that tam either on his head or tucked into his belt. The past is the past. Now we need assurances that none of your tribe will interfere with our work or intentionally damage documents belonging to the Book of Knowledge."

"I will need to persuade my people," Ruskin said. "I ask that a member of your group join me at our village. The senior grandmother Minskus must give her consent and she is not easily convinced.

"When the jury arrested Clovis from your chambers, he threatened death to anyone who would betray him. I did not have the courage to stand up and take away his power and influence. The pain of regret now runs deep."

"Do the offens have the ability to usurp power from one of their own? Where is Clovis now?" Magellan asked.

"The Court of Judgement ruled that he committed an unforgivable crime, and he was sent to prison for eternity. Rumor said he escaped on a Basque whaling ship crossing the Atlantic. A story told years later said he was killed by a hostile native for stealing."

"I pity the poor Captain that discovered him among his crew members," Magellan lamented. "Those condemned to the plank only take their curse into the ocean, so be it that his fate was determined by another nation."

"I have come to a decision," Copernicus announced. He tucked his thumbs into the pockets of his tapestry vest.

"A solution?" Gaeten asked. "Can I do my part to help?"

"Indeed. That is exactly my plan. I will negotiate with Madame Minskus and establish a rapport. Gaeten will join me, as mothers soften when they see the innocence of a boy. We'll hope for a truce and assurances of respect."

"What happens to me, Monsieur?" Ruskin asked.

"You will stay here and assist in our study halls and library, where you will learn the value of knowledge. You'll be exposed to an understanding of the world's history, its past inventions and potential for society's future.

"You will learn the consequence of deceit that results in death and despair of a nation. The oldest records are in ancient Egyptian script and are one of a kind. Our records begin with the *Book of Thoth*, deciphering the secrets and codes of the earth when Rameses ruled.

"Be wary, Ruskin, not to repeat or use any spells as they are forbidden here. It is an honor that we bestow upon you. Should you break our trust or fall under the curses, you will be banished and face a far worse fate than Clovis. The redemption of your name and your people is at stake."

"You have my word and promise," the offen said.

"Excellent. Did you know that every detail in history has a face? A place and time when man dedicated his life to make a change. You will list them all back to the Romans. Without the work we do, the world will end one day, all for naught."

"It will be my honor, Messieurs. You may remember my grandmother, Quinntella, our medicine woman. She loved working with you and keeping the cubby holes sorted. She lived over six hundred years until pirate ships came ashore and treated my people as slaves. They whipped and spat at her for being too slow. It broke her spirit —she now withers her last days in our camp."

Copernicus wiped a tear from his face. "Yes, I remember Quinn, a special lady, yet she still lingers in her misery. Move closer into the light, Ruskin, I want to look at your face. Your redemption has the ability to restore her spirit."

Ruskin eased forward and Copernicus studied his eyes.

"Oui, Monsieur Ruskin, you have your grandmother's spirit and a good heart. I believe that you will carry on in her footsteps. Perhaps it is time to put the events of Clovis and Punket in the past. Thanks to Gaeten, we have recovered what was lost and we can rebuild."

Copernicus toiled over his old memories of Quinn. She was not only an offen but she had contracted an ancient spell from Clovis. Hundreds of years before, she found Clovis one day sitting tortured by the bridge, wailing and carrying on in a rage of temper and fever. The mythology of the scorpions and serpents had taken hold of his mind, and he couldn't eat or sleep as a fire burned in his soul.

She was a strong woman and denied the evil curse bestowed on Clovis. She willed her own power to defy the spell and accept only the goodness it offered, sitting by his bed for weeks until he sat upright and famished.

His appetite was insatiable and his mind was driven to seek out the excerpts of Thoth to protect them from the scorpions. Rumor abounded later of an Egyptian temple sending emissaries to seize Clovis.

"Merci, Monsieur Copernicus, I am indebted to you for a lifetime."

A crescendo of applause erupted for Ruskin and Gaeten, and across the room, Leonardo captured the moment with his sketch pens.

"This could equal my Mona Lisa. Perhaps in time others will see the beauty and penance I've given from my heart."

"Ah, my dear Leonardo," Copernicus said with an affectionate slap on the back. "It is preserving the moment, and I thank you. Through your art, I am seeing much beauty the world bestows. You have shown me how to look at colors, objects, and expression as it touches the spirit."

An urgent curiosity brought Gaeten to Galileo's side.

"Monsieur Galileo, when I was in the caves, did you hear my heart and mind speak to you? I was trying to cultivate the gifts of magical senses. I know the nautilus provided light to my quest."

"Dear boy, you have a pure heart. As long as it remains that way, the sages have a window to your soul. Let the wisdom you acquire guide you, and never challenge what is part of history. It cannot be changed."

Gaeten knew his entire being had been elevated to a new realm of understanding.

11

Commission to the New World

Sitting on his tattered vendor's mat in the market square to sell his catch, Gaeten didn't flinch in response to the townsfolk gossiping and pointing his way.

He listened more intently to the cacophony of sounds funneling to his right ear, with the buzz of merchants bartering and criers' voices over the throngs. His acute senses were tuned to the morning noises of children running, and carriages with their heavy clomps and the drumming of hooves.

An aristocratic Madame from Dinan was gathering an audience in the market, demanding that her gossip be heard by shoppers and merchants. She paraded close enough to be overheard by Gaeten, showing off her flounce of silks and hooped skirts, lace pantaloons, and a sun parasol to protect her porcelain skin. A young servant was at her side.

"That's the lad going on an exploration with Cartier. Monsieur must have felt pity for him." A few snickers came to her satisfaction, and with delight, her volume increased.

"Yes, his father abandoned his family and was last seen on a pirate ship in the Mediterranean. The buccaneer left his urchins to public care and it's a drain on the church coffers," she said to Madame Hunalt, with disdain.

She pointed and poked her rolled fan in Gaeten's direction as she wound down.

Although Madame Cartier had told him it was rude to eavesdrop, Gaeten's ears could not deny the personal assault. Forgetting her advice, fury drove him to his feet with new courage.

"My father is *not* a pirate, and I dare you to accuse Monsieur Cartier of sowing pity on my head. Do you know how many leagues are under the ocean? Can you count to one hundred on an abacus, Madame? No, I expect that you employ yourself in gossip and disdain on innocent folks who labor to serve you and don't have the courage to tell the king he is taxing his people into the grave."

The young servant boy's eyes fell to the ground and he took a step back lest he might insult himself.

Madame stood, taken aback by the outburst, then struck out. "Such impudence, garçon. A woman of my stature has no need of an abacus such as you speak, or any spells. I can afford to employ myself in any manner that I wish. I shall ask Monsieur Hunalt to shoo you away for your rudeness and I'll ask the priest to desist in your alms."

The grand lady expected the crowd to join in belittling the lad, but instead, they looked at her as an ill-behaved child.

Madame Hunalt was abashed that she was in the path of the Dinan woman's wrath but saw the irony of the banter.

With diplomacy, she said, "Madame, we thank you for your concern about the younger generation in Saint-Malo. Young Monsieur Gaeten is a reputable merchant and deserves to have pride in his family name. He has no need for alms, and we do not share in your insults."

"Hmmph! Indignant. I'll speak my mind to Monsieur Cartier directly and demand the lad be punished. Abbott Le Veneur will be most displeased. I have good standing in France and Saint-Malo, and my words go far."

Turning around to stomp off, she plowed straight into Catherine who had heard the insults.

"Bonjours, Madame. I don't know you. Are you new to Saint-Malo? Perhaps you haven't yet met my husband's apprentice, Gaeten Mansart. We expect the king's commission shortly and I'm sure you will want to send your good wishes. If you ever need a reliable assistant for services, you'll find none better than Monsieur Mansart. Perhaps after an apology, he might see fit to be hired."

Catherine didn't lose a second of poise as she nodded to Madame Hunalt and winked to the lad, then continued on her way.

The abashed Madame from Dinan corralled her skirts and turned away in a huff leaving a waft of heavy, sweet perfume.

"Ah, Gaeten, she is from Paris, I can tell from the excess of fragrance," Madame Hunalt said. "Pay no heed to the likes of her. No matter where your father might be, your French heritage is worthy of all the king's men."

"Oui, et merci for your good words."

After the kafuffle, Gaeten was eager to dispose of his wares and get to Limoilou. Rumor at the manor was that the Abbott was bringing a formal committee including Philippe

Chabot to discuss Cartier's commission. King Francis had reviewed Jacques' cartography and navigation reports and wanted the Abbott's valued opinion.

With the last of the mussels sold to another merchant, Gaeten rolled up his mat. Stopping suddenly, a chill or omen caused the hairs on his neck to tickle his anticipation.

Everything slowed in motion and a warm wind swirled over the cobblestone courtyard. Picking up debris, a wind tunnel worked its way across the square. Its low humming was unmistakable to Gaeten, then a soft echo of his name swept through the air, repeating it over and over.

He searched for anyone that might be watching but the name became louder and the sensation stronger. He blocked out the merchants that he recognized, then the bystanders, bringing the world before him to a snail's pace. But the whispering of his name still called out.

We have a truce with the offens, and I trust Ruskin's promise.

Gaeten's thoughts drifted in confusion as he scanned the trees and lanes, stopping at a moving, dark shadow at the end of an alley.

His eyes locked on the man, wearing a sash headband and a black patch over one eye. He leaned against the wall of the butcher shop, resting on one foot.

At dawn that morning, strangers had flooded into town from a privateer ship, returning from months of plundering for fortune in the Mediterranean.

"What would a pirate want with me?" he mused.

The man stuffed rolled tobacco into his cob pipe from a pouch he drew from his pocket. When he lit his match, the light enhanced the pirate's face until he blew circles of smoke.

"Non! C'est impossible!"

Rubbing his eyes, Gaeten leered at the phantom man, this time noticing the pirate was balanced on a peg leg. The buccaneer stayed back and motioned to approach.

Stepping forward, Gaeten caught sight of Ruskin under the fish cart. The offen was huddled beside his daughter, Miradew, both siphoning kippers from the merchant's cart.

Ruskin's head turned to watch the pirate entice Gaeten, and he raised a hand of caution. Leaving the safety of the cart, he blended into the market's workings.

The pirate didn't alter his composure but continued to wait for Gaeten to come closer.

"Bonjours, Gaeten," the pirate said softly.

"How do you know my name?"

"How is your brother—Julien?" His eyes burrowed into Gaeten's soul. "Do you not know your own Papa?"

"Non, my Papa left Saint-Malo and will not return. If you find him, tell him that I take good care of Julien. I work hard and support us both. We do not need a Papa who didn't love us enough to remain when we were too young to fend for ourselves.

"We have the blood of our loving Mama who sacrificed everything she had to care for us. We did not see you come to her funeral. Do you wish to know where she is buried?"

Searching for the slightest resemblance stirred his heart and he realized the pathetic condition of the stranger. The man before him had withered in spirit and body, and Gaeten couldn't deny he felt deep sympathy.

"Do you need a meal, Monsieur? I can bring you bread and cheese."

Gaeten dug into his pocket and drew out some coins then laid them on the ground at the stranger's foot.

Ruskin had settled in an alcove to listen and guard.

Muttering to himself, he came to a conclusion.

"Copernicus said a man must fight his own battles to keep his self-respect. But also, I must come to the aid of my friends when they are in need. This would be a time when an offen might run and watch from a distance. Mais non, I will be close at hand," Ruskin assured himself.

"Do not look at your Papa as a beggar," the pirate said. "You have my blood in you and that cannot change. The Madame from Paris said that you are going on a commission soon with Jacques Cartier to the new world, n'est pas?"

"Monsieur, if you have heard that news it must be so but have no concern for me and my brother. Madame et Monsieur Cartier will ensure that we are safe. What good is a Papa with one leg who cannot even tell his own children that he loves them?"

Gaeten looked at the ground unable to bear looking into his father's eyes. "I must go, Papa, and remember that we love you, but we have no need of a pirate."

He turned and walked away slowly from the stranger as the market returned to its activities. When he looked back, the pirate and the coins were gone.

Arriving at the manor house out of breath, he felt both regret and relief from meeting his father. The sky had turned grey with the threat of rain. It would be welcome as the pastures were parched.

"Bonjours, Madame!" Gaeten beamed to see Catherine singing as she scrubbed linens in the back garden. The heavy wooden bucket was brimming with soap suds, and he lifted it closer for her.

"You have grown since yesterday," she said. "If you bring in some vegetables from the garden and a day's worth of eggs from the hen house, I will have fresh baked bread and cheese waiting in the kitchen."

Taking a basket from the planter's shed, he bounced toward a row of spring peas.

He longed to ask Madame about the rumor in town about Cartier's commission but held his tongue. When his chores were done, he returned to empty Catherine's bucket and joined her in the kitchen.

"We have good news, Gaeten. The Abbott came last night after you'd left. King Francis has offered my dear Jacques a commission to the new world. You will be going off to sea next April.

"I will leave the rest of the details for Monsieur. He is eager to tell you and is working in his library. Would you be so kind as to take him a tray and tea for his dinner?"

Knocking on the heavy mahogany doors, he waited for Cartier's voice to reply.

"Ah, I hear the footsteps of the master of the crow's nest. Come in," Cartier beckoned with a chortle.

Leaving the tray on Monsieur's desk, Gaeten scurried to the student's chair and waited.

12

Preparing the Grande Hermine

"We travel in April next. The king has granted us three ships. Grande Hermine is the largest at one hundred tonnes, Petite Hermine is sixty tonnes and Émérillon is a galleon of forty tonnes, all full masted. They are old and weathered, but with good chinking and some tarring, they will journey well. The main beams are solid timber. We will solicit crew until we have full capacity.

"Although Jean Le Veneur from the Abbey will assist in the selection of seamen from our citizens, we need a crew for preparations. The natives will be more accommodating and eager to see us if we bring gifts for trade. Verrazano said that shiny objects are a delight. So now you have facts to prove your provision requests."

Gaeten smiled to himself thinking of the similarity in the offens attraction to shiny objects as well.

"Oui, Monsieur, and much congratulations. You will be the best mariner ever from Saint-Malo, and I am greatly honored to be among your crew."

"Gaeten, you have given me encouragement and urged my spirit. You've been studious with your calculations and tendering for supplies. I am grateful to you, my young friend. We have studied the journals of explorers before us and it will be patriotic to plant the fleur-de-lis at fortresses along the great river."

As the two men reveled in their accomplishments, Cartier noticed the tray. "It seems that Madame has sent us two portions and two teacups, so let's celebrate this moment."

Gaeten eased forward to gratefully accept the tea.

"Where do the ships come from?" he asked. "I will want to help with the preparation and chinking. Monsieur Devereau taught me to chink his cottage on the hillside. We prepared oakum, gathered moss and goat dung and an assortment of animal hairs, then a coating of tar. We will need much more for three ships."

"The ships come this fall, as the leaves change and the north wind blows. The Grande Hermine is our flagship, and we will work over the winter . . . and we must keep the goats busy."

The two sipped in silence, envisioning the miracle to come to Saint-Malo's harbor. In their visions, the seas were calm and the masts fully open as the trio of galleons glided across the Atlantic under golden sunrises.

Catherine's brother-in-law, Thomas Fromont was appointed ship-master of the Grande Hermine, Jacques Maingate commanded the Petite Hermine, and Mace Jalobert piloted the Courlieu, the alias of the Émérillon.

"The pilot of the main ship will be my dear friend Jehann Poulet, yet we need many more."

"I recall Monsieur Jalobert from an occasion when I was studying here at the manor. It will be a comfort to Madame that you travel with trusted friendship."

"Oui, that is so."

"I have many questions about life at sea," Gaeten said.

"The routines on the king's ships start with morning prayers for safe travel and guidance. Everyone attends unless the priest deems the person too ill to leave the sickbay. A jailor and monitor will maintain stringent rules for the crew to keep the ship tight. Chaplain Le Breton will make sure we have Bibles onboard."

Gaeten took the tea in two swallows and gobbled down his bread and cheese. He was burning with passion to return to his studies with the visionaries.

Word spread quickly through the town, and eager volunteers enlisted for work on land now and at sea later. Even maimed warriors returning from the battlefields were eager to find a bit of work.

Gaeten found he could loiter unnoticed while sweeping at the drink houses, and he thrived on seafaring stories of sailors and pirates. As it was the hub for the town's gossip and communication, he couldn't afford to be absent. However, when he didn't earn a wink to stay, he was swatted out by the innkeeper.

Habitually and with a sense of longing, he scanned the tavern for the one-legged pirate.

With the fishing season diminishing, Gaeten had more time to work on the ship, loading provisions. Julien assumed his chores at the livery, and Catherine assured him she would oversee his brother while he was away.

The masters grilled him over and over about the routes and his calculations while they challenged and cautioned.

"You realize, Gaeten, that telepathically we will travel with you on your explorations with Cartier. Remember that your gifts are meant to guide and protect you." Galileo said.

"I'll never forget. Also, Ruskin has volunteered as a stowaway to back me up."

"We're glad of that, but don't be naïve to think that an offen has no powers. Some folks don't believe in nymphs and offens, and others fear them saying they have bad magic. Look beyond what you see and rely on the soul within.

"Your journey will become part of our journals' recording history. We will eagerly await your return. Your official report will be entered in the annals of time."

Standing back listening, Leonardo stroked his beard and labored over borrowed wisdom.

"Gaeten, you hear from us our hopes and dreams for the future. We put a great burden on you, yet I should remind you of a Biblical parable that applies to your journey and the achievements that await you."

"Oui, Master da Vinci, which parable is that? My dear mother read to me from the holy book at bedtime."

"This parable is about five talents—we are born with unique talents, some prolific and indelible and others harbored within. The master goes on a journey and must leave his property in the care of others. He chooses three men. To the first, he leaves five talents, to the second only two, and to the third man, only one. Do you recall what happens?"

Gaeten didn't want to falter before his seers. "Please refresh my memory, Monsieur da Vinci."

"On his return, the master calls the three servants. The first invested well and used his five talents to grow his crops and provide food and water to his village. He offers the master ten talents as a return, and the master is pleased. The second also invested well and returns four talents for the two he received, again pleasing the master. The third man steps forward, feeling secure that he has protected the one talent he was given and offers it back. The master is displeased. What is the lesson, Gaeten?"

"It is the right of each person to use his resources for good, to benefit himself and others. It didn't matter to the master if he gave five talents or two, those servants were prudent caretakers of the talents. But the third man did not allow his gift to prosper. You have reminded me of my responsibility for being chosen."

"The responsibility in life is great," Leonardo said.

"Merci, mes amis, you have bestowed upon me a great honor and trust. I promise that my eyes and ears will be yours. The wind will carry the sound of my voice, and my sight will travel in dreams. Yet my spirit is everywhere you wish it to be."

Gaeten was dismissed for the evening, but as he neared the exit, he heard a whisper.

"Yes, we chose well!"

In the days up to April 20, 1534, much ado was underway at the harbor as the last-minute preparations escalated. Gaeten began to rely on his steadfast accomplice Ruskin, who was nearby whenever he needed assistance.

In the morning hours before Cartier's first commission set sail from Saint-Malo, Gaeten's acute hearing tuned in on the weight of the heavy fog, hearing the altered tone of the church bells pealing across the countryside.

At last, the three galleons began their crossing of the Atlantic, destined for the waters of the great St. Lawrence passage. Stretching seventy feet in length, the Grande Hermine was considered a small ship and was accompanied immediately by her sister vessel. Both had three giant flax-cloth square sails on each mast including the masthead, two crow's nests, and a spire at the bow with the furled flag of the fleur-de-lis.

Standing at the helm, Jacques Cartier watched until Catherine was barely visible as a dot on the pier. The crew was fully occupied pulling in ropes and anchors and securing stores, but Jacques' eyes remained on Catherine. Gaeten sat high in the crow's nest watching the land below fade to become a memory.

While the others in town dispersed back through cobblestone streets to their homes, Catherine and Julien focused on the horizon until there was nothing but blue sky.

Sitting on nearby abandoned crates within sight of Julien was a peg-legged crippled pirate with pride in his heart and a withered body that harbored too many regrets. His youngest son was only feet away but the barrier was too great.

The masted carrack, with Cartier and one hundred men from Saint-Malo, continued beyond the rocky island at the mouth of the Rance Estuary and disappeared past the ramparts. The seas that day were calm with enough of a wind to set an easy pace.

13

Sighting of New Found Land

Gaeten inspected every inch of the Grande Hermine, running his hand along the railing and counting the deck planks. He rechecked the ropes and measured the height of each mast until he felt a union with the ship.

This was the first occasion for Gaeten to leave French soil and the people he had been familiar with during his young years.

The excitement and revelry of departure could not replace the memories of his family and friends, yet now it was only the mariners. No seers, no Catherine, no Julien, no Hunalt family—only Ruskin, and the talisman in his pocket.

"What is this ache in my heart?"

As routine and the rigors of the sea set in rapidly with a bustle of activity, Gaeten felt absorbed into the ship. Cartier, his captains, and the first mates were focused on maps and the horizon until the third day when they called upon his expertise.

"Gaeten, come down from there," Jehann Poulet barked as he scowled at the crow's nest.

"Oui, Monsieur."

In three swoops, Gaeten was directly in front of the first mate on the main deck.

"Ahoy there, Gaeten, you have made yourself scarce. Meet directly with the provisions master regarding your calculations."

That night as the sun settled, he rapped his knuckles on the captain's cabin where he had been invited for a drink.

"Permission to enter, Capitaine?"

"The sun has set, Monsieur Mansart, and I wish you to show me more of the constellation you have studied. Catherine told me that when I look upon the stars, I will feel her heart across the miles. Is that so?"

"Oui, Monsieur, you see the North Star? That is Polaris and the center of the heavens. Wait a minute until the clouds pass and you will see."

Cartier extended the sextant for a clearer view.

"Madame will be watching Polaris from the manor terrace so you see your souls are in unity. While we watch the stars, the world moves and rotates. Columbus was correct."

At the end of the second week, the ship met her first gale and Gaeten had the grueling test of manning the upper masts against ferocious waves and winds. Whitecaps swelled above the deck, threatening to swallow the bobbing ships.

"I had not imagined that my stomach would want to leave my body in this way! Mon Dieu, it is not pleasant."

Ruskin was in the lower basket holding fast to the great hemp ropes and rigging. Across from Gaeten was a second operator on the shorter masts, Guillaume from Dieppe, who was experienced with tacking on the Atlantic.

Through the gusting rain, they lost contact with the smaller ships. Clasping the amulet, Gaeten closed his eyes and listened, letting the waves bring the pleas to his ears as the stinging salt besieged him.

It was faint at first, then began with a soft humming. Although he could not see the amplified acoustics, the ocean came to his ears, and he heard Jalobert command his crew to prepare to abandon ship.

"Do you hear the other ships as I do, Ruskin?"

Ruskin was pale and tense from holding tight on the ropes. "I was focused on the crow's nest but when the wind came up this morning, I heard the humming as a warning."

"I sensed that as well," Gaeten said. "It's the unspoken warning from nature. The worst fear is upon the Petite Hermine and the Émérillon."

Fear of the inevitable was growing in Gaeten's eyes. Feeling helpless, he confided his fears to Poulet.

"Non, non, Monsieur Mansart, it is impossible that you have heard such distress. We have not yet heard the signal of the canon."

Poulet reported the concern to Cartier, who remained on the bridge, studying the shadows fading on the horizon. The burden of three ships was great on his shoulder.

"Do not question Mansart, Jehann. The boy has a gift of knowing. Whatever he hears is true—be prepared to rescue."

No one ate that day or night beyond a glass of red wine and hard biscuits for sustenance. In spite of the tossing sea, Gaeten climbed to the crow's nest where he felt closer to the masters and the constellations. As dark clouds passed, he waited until the North Star became a beacon. On an imaginary abacus, he counted the degrees between him and Polaris and felt stabilized.

When the sea calmed, Cartier mustered him. "Gaeten, before I left, my dear wife told me I should heed your special gifts of exceptional senses. The details of how this came about are not important, but I would like to know if you have gleaned critical data."

"Oui, Monsieur, the wind has sent messages from the other commanders, with the acoustics carried over the water like an echo. I see faint silhouettes lingering behind yet they are moving. The Émérillon is taking on water and they have trouble making repairs. Monsieur Jalobert fears he cannot keep up."

Cartier did not challenge the boy's theory.

"Have the signalman send a message with the talking flags," he barked at the shipmaster. "The Petite Hermine will drop back in our sights. If the leaking is severe, Jalobert will rescue the crew of the Émérillon. The main ship will forge ahead as planned and wait at the great banks for the others, then we'll lower the longboats."

Cartier returned to Gaeten. "Bless you for your gifts. Let me know when you have a further sense of danger. It is a hard day, but we have survived and we will sup tonight."

Gaeten gave a mariner's salute. "Oui, Capitaine Cartier."

The captain's quarters had a strong similarity to his library at Limoilou. Maps were spread on the tall desks, and scrolls of maps and journals were tucked into cubby holes. The astrolabe, compass, traverse boards, sextants, depth monitors, and barometers were at his fingertips, and he constantly studied his readings of longitude and latitude.

Cartier and the first mate were concerned about the slow progress and pored over statistics with the shipmaster.

With a spool of rope, Gaeten made a chip log to measure knots at defined intervals. When dropped off the stern, the weights measured the ship's speed. Using Cartier's quill pen, he recorded in the navigation logs.

With flourishing respect, Fromont, the shipmaster, addressed the boy, "According to these maps, we should sight land sometime tomorrow. Gaeten, have you seen any Basque ships looking for the rocky island? The Vikings will start an early harvest for whales' blubber."

"I've kept a sextant to my eyes all day. Late this afternoon, a foggy blur on the horizon could have been a distant ship. I made the notation on the charts. Calculations tell us that if the sky is clear, I'll find land on the horizon by noon tomorrow."

Cartier sighed. "Then we are on course to equal Verrazano's log to the great seaway. Perhaps tomorrow we will go ashore at the auck land and hunt from the skies as we could use relief for our dwindling food supplies."

"Will we find fish too, Sir?"

"Oh yes, my boy. I've heard of the cod running so thick that they can ground any ship. Surely we will find them soon and be able to feast. We must ready the salt barrels. If the soil is as good as the harbors, we will see blessings."

The shipmaster interjected, "The priest reports that seven men in sickbay are suffering from ague and rickets. We gave each of them an extra ration portion for strength and some medicinal brandy."

"It will be good to put solid ground under our feet again," Cartier said. "If Stadacona has no natives, we can set up a camp and store food. It won't be easy as the coast is rocky and barren.

"Oui, I remember you saying it was Cain's land." The boy recited.

Cartier smiled as he recalled his words.

Gaeten, Guillaume and Ruskin were allotted space in a corner below deck on canvas slings with barely enough room to wiggle.

The smell of decay, animals, sweat and the sea was in Gaeten's bed and his skin as he wrote in his journal by candlelight.

My thoughts go to Limoilou and the sages watching the heavens from the belfry. Perhaps they no longer think of me and have found another protégé and experiments to occupy their thoughts. Galileo assured me that if I kept a pure heart, the sages could see into my soul. My thoughts beseech them to send me the comfort of their presence.

Groaning, snoring and bodily noises from the crew kept him from slumber. Hours later, the watchman descended the ladder to check the cargo. Gaeten's eyes were accustomed to shadows in the darkness, and when the light swooped across the bales of goods, he saw a stubby ankle protruding from the sacks.

The watchman saw it too and grabbed at the scruff of a stowaway as a pair of rats scurried from their roost.

Ruskin peered intently at the whimpering scruff being hauled to the main deck and Gaeten wondered if he heard a slight humming.

"Did you bring another offen on board, Ruskin?"

"Not by my knowledge, my friend. But I know this young offen, it is clear from his stature he is related to my tribe. He must have followed me. What will happen to the offender?"

The stowaway protested vigorously with his feet kicking and was hauled up the ladder. Gaeten realized by the offen's smooth face that he was young, but he admired his gusto. Grossly thin and trembling, the lad declared himself a Frenchmen nonetheless.

"Merci, merci, do not throw me overboard . . . I cannot swim. I will surely die and come back to haunt you in your dreams."

"The Grande Hermine already has a contingent in sickbay, so Capitaine will be able to place you with rigorous work," the watchman muttered.

In the morning, the sheepish dwarfed offen was scrubbing the decks. He was timid when asked his given name but was referred to by the crew as Oursin, a word they knew meant urchin.

From the crow's nest, Gaeten watched him curiously and felt a kinship.

Galileo, is this what you have sent me to assure me of your support, another offen?

With his assignment of labor, Oursin carried hints of fury in his dark eyes and cursed under his breath while avoiding Ruskin.

The landing of the longboats would prove to be treacherous on the rocky shores. Gaeten overheard the plan to send young Oursin to test the waters, assessing him as expendable.

The boat pilot tossed a line to the surprised lad.

"Oursin! We are near enough to anchor. Go off the bow with the tether. It is clear that the rocks below will jut and cut your feet, so be warned."

The fearful stowaway prepared to dive as instructed when Gaeten jumped up to join him.

The pilot was angered. "Gaeten! You have not been given that order."

From his fishing skills in Saint-Malo, Gaeten was accustomed to rocky debris and boulders. In an instant, Oursin was lifeless in the water with blood oozing from his head, midway between the longboat and a large, smooth boulder.

Lashing the tow-line under his arms, Gaeten cupped his hand under Oursin's chin and swam toward the boulder. After a few gasps of fresh air, Oursin began to thrash.

Gaeten whispered gently, "Oursin, you are safe. Don't fight me. Did Galileo send you?"

Oursin said. "The science father took me from under the fish cart. I can't swim . . . the elders knew that, why did they send me?"

"Yet you are saved as fate has willed. You have a mission to fulfill—Ruskin will mentor you."

He raised the small offen up to the boulder, leaving him sprawled on his side to recover. Behind, the pilot was cursing and swearing at the pair for their disregard of orders.

Gaeten lashed the tow-line and tightened the pull until the longboat acquiesced and followed. A shadow caught his eye, as Ruskin was there too and had taken up the slack.

After weeks of fishing from the longboats, the landing parties took to the rocky slopes to shoot auks—large, meaty birds that could only fly short distances and were easy prey.

The slaughter of birds and roar of muskets echoed inland, raising the curiosity of local tribes about the ships and crew.

For a time, the natives watched from the bushes, as these strange men fired their sticks into the air. Puffs of magic, black smoke rose above, bagging another auck.

The natives were angered but waited. The Micmac chief cautioned his braves, "These strangers disturb our hunting grounds and make angry noise into the sky. They do not respect the laws of nature and the survival of man and animal, be wary of their fire sticks."

Standing on the rocky slopes with the longboat crew, Gaeten's intense vision caught sight of tribesmen watching from the bush.

"Oursin, keep to your task. Curiosity is not to be feared. They intend no harm or we would not be standing here. Find your inner courage."

"Who is curiosity?"

Gaeten smiled at the offen's naiveté. "You'll have many years to learn. It is not a person. Curiosity is a friend in your thoughts. It's the desire 'to know' that you were born with."

The wastefulness and gluttony of the white men appalled the natives, who valued the bounty of Mother Earth.

In July, the shipmaster ordered that the cannons be tested, startling the natives with their powerful boom.

The next day, the crew had their first tribal sighting in a large bay. A contingent of caribou-skin canoes strategized, then charged forward to intimidate the newcomers. Cartier knew them to be Micmacs of the birch bark wigwam villages cited by earlier explorations.

Gaeten was enthralled to observe the braves, some in moose skin breeches, and many bare-chested with necklaces made of leather, with animal claws, and carved bones draped over them. Many had dark black braids anchored by headbands, with colorful bird feathers trailing behind.

But it was the color of their skin that captivated the young mariner, as other foreigners that visited Saint-Malo had been fair-skinned.

"Lower the head mast, but remain in the crow's nest," the shipmaster bellowed.

Cartier ordered several longboats to be lowered to go and greet the natives with gifts of friendship and a white truce flag. The captain himself stood tall at the bow as they plied the waters toward the canoes.

The Micmac Chief Panounais was leery about the newcomers and raised his hand for a standoff, letting each leader make assessments. With the imposing power of the ships shadowing over them, the chief conceded they were outnumbered.

Cartier brought along a lad from Italy, who had journeyed with Verrazano and could translate with the Micmac in words and sign language.

Once it was clear that Cartier's men and ships meant no harm, the Micmacs were ready to negotiate. The Micmac communities each revered their own saqamaw for wisdom and leadership.

Stepping forward with the chief was their saqamaw warrior, Henri Membertou, a powerfully tall man, a respected leader, and a medicine man. Membertou was intensely curious about Cartier's voyage and the new people with hats that wished to settle on their land.

Pointing at Cartier's plumed hat, Chief Panounais gestured that it would fit himself, and from the crow's nest, Gaeten snickered at the sight of the chief in the Parisian fashion accessory.

In the spirit of friendship, the Micmacs offered fine beaver pelts. The crew of the Hermine brought colored glass baubles, silver trinkets, and shiny mirrors to tantalize the natives.

It was comical to Gaeten to watch the natives' awe as they discovered their own faces in the mirrors. Listening to the meeting's progress with acute skills, he memorized details to report and etch in the journals for the seers.

The landing party followed Membertou and the Micmacs to their village at the mouth of the St. Lawrence for a pow-wow. Cartier's men removed their boots and sat cross-legged in a circle with their native friends. In an exchange of gifts, a gleaming, polished copper kettle was offered to the saqamaw in appreciation.

Sharing a peace pipe of bitter tobacco, the crew suffered headaches, and regretfully, the reciprocal gift of French brandy caused a euphoric reaction for the Micmacs.

As some Micmacs lapsed into stupors with incoherent babbling, Panounais became wary of the newcomers' intentions and sent them to return to their anchor.

Cartier's translator promised to be back with more gifts and to hire inland guides. Still wearing his plumed hat, the Chief nodded in agreement.

As the crew returned guardedly to the ship, Gaeten listened and watched the Micmacs through the sextant. Although not a trained translator, he was able to interpret their reactions and hand gestures.

In the darkness, Cartier's men had not noticed that the shiny buckles had been removed from their shoes as they sat in friendship.

Gaeten laughed to himself. "The Micmacs and the offens have a lot in common," he whispered alone. But a shiver ran up his spine.

"All is not well with the Micmacs."

With the return of the last longboat, he saw an object in floating the water. Peering closer, it was a familiar slouch hat with gold braiding. Close by, arms flailing out of control the offen floated, with his head bobbing and then sinking.

"Man overboard! Shipmaster Fromont, it's Ruskin. He's drowning and desperate!"

"What is he doing in the drink?" Fromont shouted.

A crush of mariners rushed to the edge with a rescue line of heavy knotted hemp and tossed it into the surf.

"Take it, Ruskin," Gaeten called. "Hold the rope."

"I can't swim." His head bobbed more, taking in gulps of seawater.

Skilled with diving, from fishing and finding barnacles on the rocky banks, Gaeten asked, "Monsieur Capitaine, I can dive. May I go and get him?"

Cartier was astounded. "I can't risk losing you too."

"I intend to have many years as a mariner, Monsieur, I would not give that up for anything."

The shipmaster balked. "It's too risky, you'll drown too."

Gaeten looked again at his mentor then at the helpless offen slipping under the surf.

"I need permission. He has little time left."

Wasting no time, Cartier conceded. "Fromont, see that Gaeten is firmly attached to the rope and rescue board."

Looking down, he whispered. "You come back. That is an order."

Gaeten miscalculated the depth from the ship's railing to the surf below and entered the water gasping for air. Not looking back, he gripped the float board and dove through the waves with the rope trailing.

Ruskin was no longer in sight, but a ring of air bubbles gave his location.

Gaeten waved the drifting hat to a landing boat being rowed his way with a rescue crew. Taking a long breath of air, he slipped under the surf for what seemed to be a death sentence. Cartier feared the worst as he watched from the bridge, swinging a lantern for light.

Suddenly a torrent of water exploded, bringing up Ruskin by the collar of his shirt, with Gaeten thrusting his arm over him. Wrapping the hemp around his upper body, Gaeten signaled to begin a tow. He knew his strength was waning and he was in imminent peril himself.

Then he heard the voice of Galileo speak to his soul as if carried in the wind.

"Remember, Gaeten, that you have the power to save and protect yourself and others. All that you need is inside."

A surge of adrenaline enabled him to grab the second rescue line to pull himself to the rowboat. Guillaume was one of the rescuers and pulled him over the side.

"Gaeten, you obstinate fool, you half-drowned."

"Monsieur Gilly, how dare you to accuse me of that?"

Gaeten showed a row of pearly whites. "Heroism is the right of a Frenchman when you value the lives of friends above your own," he said. "You sleep well at night with that in your heart."

Gasping and choking, Ruskin was carried to the sick bay and warmed with a dose of brandy. Gaeten insisted on sitting by him through the night.

"Ruskin, my dear friend, how did you end up in the ocean? Oursin told me that offens can't swim."

"He was right. But because I am different than all the other crew members, I needed to prove my worth. My intention was to follow as a spy and even seek out more of my people here perhaps, but I missed departing on the landing boat. It was selfish of me that you needed to risk yourself."

"We are different in various ways, Ruskin, but appearances are the least of our attributes. Galileo reminded me while I was in the drink that our qualities are unseen but no less worthy."

The old offen tried to make light of his regrets. "Your words are kind and wise for your age, Gaeten. It is too bad that you don't get to live seven hundred years like the offens."

Passing the sickbay, Cartier overheard their discussion. He closed his eyes. "Ruskin is a most peculiar comrade for Gaeten."

14

The First Winter

In the following months, Cartier's expedition ventured to Stadacona, not far down the St. Lawrence, where his men built a thirty-foot cross for France.

The autumn winds were blowing, and Cartier started plans for his return to Saint-Malo as their supplies were insufficient to make it through the winter months. The leaves of the great maples and oaks were beginning to yellow—the clock of the season.

Regretfully, he decided the Émérillon was not seaworthy enough for the journey back to France, so he rallied a land crew to stay over the winter until he could return.

They would remain on the boat as long as possible, but had permission to dismantle building supplies for a settlement under the French flag. A crew of carpenters was overseen by Messieurs Sequart, Esnault, Dabin, Jehan du

Mort and a half-dozen skilled craftsmen from Saint-Malo. All the crew, including Gaeten, Oursin, and the crow's nest boys went to work making repairs, with daily foraging on land for supplies to prepare the abandoned ship.

Tired from a long day in the woods, Gaeten crowded close to the campfire for warmth, with his feet numb from the cold. Before leaving Saint-Malo, each crewman was given spare socks and warned that they must be washed only in rainwater. But Gaeten had lazily washed his with seawater, and painful welts now covered his feet.

He dared not admit to his folly. For relief, he slipped away from camp to soak his wounded feet in a nearby freshwater creek. As he settled on the bank, the bushes rustled and the ripples in the water changed to a gentle, restless wake.

Before fear could overtake him, he reached for the talisman. Hot in his pocket, the amulet was pulsing against his body. He was about to call out to one of the sages when he felt a powerful surge of his inner strength.

In the darkness, two pairs of yellowish-green eyes glowed at him from barely fifteen feet away. In a panic, he froze, assessing and grasping the reality of the danger facing him.

"These are feral animals and I'm their feast."

Closing his eyes, he willed his fear to the sages. A burst of wind encircled him and he felt the presence of Galileo and an echo of indecipherable sounds but knew the answer himself.

"Where there is one or two, there are that many more. Use your strength and show no fear—raise the amulet as your sword."

Adrenaline invaded Gaeten's stature as he rose to his feet. He puffed and growled, shining the glowing amulet as he marched in long strides toward the aggressors.

"Be gone before I call upon the invincible Ickty and Leviathan. Surely they will devour you. We are equal foes and I have no fear of you."

The wolves cowered and whimpered, before scampering back into the darkness of the forest. Calmness rewarded Gaeten's inward resources and he thought only of the seers as the wind subsided.

In spite of a truce with the Iroquois, the Stadacona fortress was manned from turrets in each corner in case of an ambush from any angle.

Weeks in the woods were productive, chopping pines, maples, and cedars to construct crude fortresses at the two sights. With native-style traverses, they dragged lumber by oxen they brought from France. Hastily, they felled and hewed great pines as the brisk winds battled their efforts.

Gaeten felt his shoulder muscles like never before as he swung the ax and took his turn at the great saw. His hands blistered and the aching of labor was unbearable, but Ruskin stood by him, reminding him of his great purpose.

"A single stroke is an accomplishment and we will try for one more, mon ami. We are expected to give our all."

At the lumber camp, the two stretched out on their backs under the stars searching for Polaris and solace. Commiserating over the day, Gaeten allowed the searing pain to ease from his thoughts. Slumber came quickly and the sun rose too soon.

Convincing an Iroquois village to offer guides to come with him to the settlement at Hochelaga, Cartier left the Stadacona party before winter settled.

A difficulty arose for Cartier's ships as they arrived at Hochelaga, with the early onset of cold that froze the St.

Lawrence. Slabs of ice gathered around the hulls until they couldn't move anymore.

Cartier decided they would have to winter at Hochelaga, and others would go back to Stadacona. Gaeten remained at Hochelaga with the two offens, Ruskin and Oursin.

Whenever trudging through the bush, he refused to wear a woolen hat in case it would interfere with his senses of sight and sound. Gaeten was ridiculed by crewmen when he relented to tying a red, woolen scarf around his forehead as a flag in the woods. The group remained under Micmac surveillance who also found amusement in his unusual attire.

Every crewman was expected to contribute by snaring a rabbit, wild grouse, squirrel or anything edible for the nightly stew. Ruskin had a hard time accepting the circle of life as he had been a farmer and fisherman in Saint-Malo.

"Ahoy, Ruskin, it is the plan of the world to survive. Here, I will show you how to build a trap. It will be swift and the hare feels nothing. We have no choice but to show Captain Cartier that we are worthy hunters."

Whittling on a strip of cedar, Gaeten planted the snare and tied it to a small tree. "I will do it as you say, Gaeten, but I will not eat of this poor animal."

"Then you will not eat."

Obstinance gave way to hunger on the second night as the rabbit juices sizzled on spits over the fire. Ruskin and Oursin tore into the white meat feasting until they could eat no more.

"Yes, Ruskin we will learn to be good hunters and take our skills back to our village in Saint-Malo." Oursin wiped the back of his sleeve across his mouth.

The crew scavenged and foraged new flavors and nutrition, with mushrooms and morels, acorns, chestnuts, autumn wild berries, nettles, and other herbs they found on the forest floor.

Without a native guide at Hochelaga, the mariners were not safe in the woods, and in the autumn, several of the crew died at the hands of Iroquois arrows.

Cartier looked for the Micmac saqamaw, Membertou, for advice and warning, but weeks would go by without having him in their sight. The genial tribesman had become a valuable translator and confidant who taught the lads to build their own canoes and snowshoes.

Disease became their greatest enemy, as the Grande Hermine's doctor battled to save the crew suffering from rickets, scurvy, and effects of starvation. Blaming the newcomers for the affliction of diseases, the Iroquois sent out raiding parties to warn them away from the settlements.

The apothecary mixed concoctions of ointments from radish root, garlic, mustard, and herbs he found in the ship's supplies. Gaeten, Oursin, Ruskin and Étienne Noël delivered experimental doses to the most severely afflicted.

The noble Captain refused his dose as did the medic troop. But at the end of the day, when Gaeten returned the ointment pot to the apothecary, he realized he had a smear of the dose on his hand. With soreness in his swollen feet, he applied the dose and sensed relief.

The doctor reported sadness. "We must bury another, mon Capitaine. The ague is most painful and contagious. How do the natives survive without getting rickets?"

Oursin asked of Ruskin, "Dear brother, we once had the plague attack our village. It was devastating but old n made a potion from herbs and weeds. She sent us to find turmeric, bilberry, and hawthorn to make a strong tea to fortify us."

"Yes, I remember the plague—so many were taken to their graves. I will ask the wise sages to send the secret in my dreams."

Gaeten overheard. "Ruskin do you also hear from the sages without sound or sight?"

Keeping his voice low, Ruskin said, "Deep within me harbors a sea of angst and urging. I can sense my time in the tunnels and the wisdom comes to me in that memory."

Gaeten nodded to himself in satisfaction. "The three of us have reached a new understanding of reliance on one another and on the wisdom of the sages."

Concerned about winter scurvy and the crew's survival, Cartier sought help from Donnaconna for secret cures. With urgency, they planned a foraging party led by the chief's son to gather ingredients for the cauldron cure. The doctor was elated to receive hope at last.

"Anything is worth a try," Cartier ordered. "Jalobert, take a party to the woods for medicinal bark and roots. Any relief to our suffering crew is worthy."

Gaeten's hand waved to volunteer. "I will go, Monsieur Jalobert."

Wearing snowshoes and Copernicus' leather boots, Gaeten and five others followed Jalobert, Domagaya, and the guide to the forest to collect the medicinal harvest.

Ruskin was at Gaeten's side at the outset, but disappeared to camouflage himself in the woods, soon reappearing with a bag of rabbit, winter partridge, acorns, walnuts, a red fox and a sack of cedar and balsam sprigs.

"Ruskin, which of your talents did you employ to deceive your prey?" Gaeten asked.

"It's not magic, but a simple snare." With the round cedar strap, he orchestrated a sudden snap, and the two broke a hearty laugh. "C'est complete." The young offen, Oursin, watched with widened eyes.

Domagaya, the chief's son, led them to a row of white cedar trees yet to be stripped of their bark. Below the permafrost, they dug out spiders' roots.

"That is the medicine that keeps the natives from suffering the bone illness," Ruskin declared. "My ancestors would have benefited from this remedy. My grandmother prepared a paste for tea from mustard, berries, honey, and dandelions."

Domagaya summoned Henri Membertou, who silently appeared from the forest. He was extraordinarily large for a Micmac and soft-spoken; not yet an ancient elder, he appeared ageless in appearance.

"I'll take the harvest back to camp," Membertou said. "These will be boiled and ladled into clay cups so everyone has a share. Nature will provide healing for the ailing. Ruskin, tell me your ancient grandmother's paste recipe."

"Grand-mère Quinntella is wise as you are, Monsieur. Secrets of medicine and life are in her head, but I watch and learn. The mystery of well-being is the yellow mustard weed, with tiny buds that we grind to a powder then she concocts a plaster that stinks. I'll search with you in the spring."

His voice pitched high as he plugged his nose about the paste's intense odor, and Oursin let out a childish laugh.

"Ha, ha, if it smells bad it is good," Membertou said.

"I may be able to find a tasting from our cook on board," Gaeten said. "The leaves are edible also and will enhance the vineyard crop. We grow it near Dijon in France."

"Vineyard crop?"

"Yes . . . grapes."

Gaeten gestured that he was sipping something delicious. "It is essential to the wines we brought as gifts."

With laughter, Membertou and Ruskin talked about gardens and herbs and concocting teas. The face of the great saqamaw showed a peaceful countenance. He had wandered many winters and seen other explorers come to his hunting grounds, scattering his people.

More than fifty natives died in the winter, and in spite of the medicinal teas, natives contracted the ague that they believed came from the white men.

The quarantine mission produced some successes for Cartier's crew, with the suffering diminished. Preserved wine bottles were filled with the remaining potion to be designated for the return voyage.

Meanwhile, the Iroquois harbored vengeance against the explorers and the Huron for encroaching on their lands and spreading disease. As a statement of might, Cartier's ship fired a warning cannon above the Iroquois encampment and the raiding parties ceased.

Returning to the ice-locked vessels with a new scheme, the crew created a ruse to create banging noises giving the pretense that they had many more able-bodied men to defend them. Even the sickest pounded the walls from their beds.

Cartier's land crew encountered Chief Donnacona in the woods with his sons Domagaya and Taignoagy.

This time, Gaeten was alarmed to sense new hostility from Donnacona. Encountering the genial Membertou, he recruited his help. Discreetly, the pair huddled in the hearing range of the tribal campfire while the chief laid plans to deceive Cartier with an ambush and massacre.

Donnacona raised his spear in anger. "The white man was here before. The Englishman, Cabot, had promised allegiance to the Iroquois, but the Frenchmen deny our nations' supremacy. We invite them with the pretense of a treaty, but we must create our own solutions.

"They bring us evil spells and disease then take from our land. It must stop. Even the deer are accustomed to their muskets and we cannot surprise our prey with our arrows. If the white men don't leave, we'll do whatever we must to protect our hunting grounds and villages."

Gaeten's heart pounded as he pressed his body against a giant maple. Donnacona raised his hand for silence at the sounds of a stranger. It was Taignoagy, listening with his ear to the ground for movements outside the camp.

Releasing Membertou of his loyalty, Gaeten held the powerful talisman tightly willing to be invisible as the tribesman poked in the shrubbery around him. Fearing that the beating of his heart could be heard, he didn't flinch as the tip of Taignoagy's spear scraped his shoulder.

Searching for a sign of Ruskin, he closed his eyes, awaiting capture. Instead, a ferocious wind gust swept over the village and suffocated their campfire.

"Was that my will . . . or the talisman? Was it Ruskin? Are the seers showing me the way to survive?"

Creeping back to Cartier's camp, he told of the planned ambush, with details of the village's location, its size in warriors and the surrounding embankments.

"That was risky and dangerous, Gaeten. You should not have been there alone."

"I knew I was safe, Monsieur, the honorable saqamaw Membertou was with me."

"Even the most stalwart must be guarded and logical in the face of opposition. Do not venture away again without a scout. Now see the doctor as your shoulder is bleeding."

"I only intended to treat my sore feet but I am aware that the consequences were not thoroughly considered."

"Nonetheless, you have done me a great service in warning us of the ambush. Your carelessness is our savior, however, the cost on another day might be your own life. Remember, Gaeten, that we are limited to our wisdom in the face of death. Use it with caution."

Gaeten accepted the reprimand as a soldier. The medic attended to the blood running down his arm and the pain in his shoulder. Grimacing, he caught sight of Ruskin climbing the mast. A subtle salute was exchanged.

Cartier refused Donnacona's offer of a treaty meeting that night, and the crew kept a vigil for an ambush in the darkness. Intercepting the sounds of animals bleating, Ruskin knew them as the tribal signals for a retreat.

"They are retreating to their camp."

In October, the French planned a deception to trap the Iroquois chief, Donnacona, and kidnap his two sons. A peace meeting was arranged for Cartier and the chief at Stadacona. A backup crew led by Jalobert watched from the woods for a violent betrayal.

At the teepee village, Cartier's group was provided luxurious lodgings. The fragrance of burning pine filled the air from the campfire, and the smell of roasting venison emanated from the hearth. The women offered flatbread and wooden bowls of corn and cooked meats.

The crew settled cross-legged in a circle and the parley began with gifts from the French, conciliatory to the Iroquois. Donnacona eyed every man with suspicion before he stuffed tobacco into the peace pipe. He puffed once each to the spirits of the East, South, West, and North Winds.

Cartier repeated the puffs and passed the pipe to the crew and braves, each blowing a mouthful of smoke into the face of the next guest as a gesture of friendship.

A chanting lament broke the silence as the revered Medicine Man danced and sang prayers to honor the heavenly spirits, an homage to the gods of fire, water and the fruits of the earth.

Membertou's passion sang to the spirits, "Ly O lay ale loya…Ly O lay ale loya." With soft, rhythmic stomping steps and an eagle-feathered staff and a bracelet of bear claws rattling in his hand, he danced until the crew was almost hypnotized.

Cartier rose and bowed with a tip of his hat.

"It is an honor to be in the company of great Iroquois Chiefs and their Medicine Man today, but the stars have signaled it is time to return to our camp. We want many months and years of peace and prosperity between our people, with respect for the traditions of the natives of Stadacona."

Donnacona, wearing Cartier's original plumed hat, signaled to his sons to rise.

"I agree to allow my brave sons to go back to Saint-Malo on the return journey." He paused in long thought. "You will give my sons education and treat them well. I wish that they learn your customs and language and bring back knowledge to our people."

"I give you my word. I will take them to the king's palace where they will live as guests of King Francis. We will take a translator of your choice and, in return, I'll leave some talented crew to integrate into the Iroquois village to learn your ways and we will defend your village against Agona."

Donnacona's sons showed reticence but acquiesced. Domagaya, the elder son, held his head high, not daring to show disappointment, but the ire of the younger Taignoagy was visible on his face and neck.

He refused to look at either his father or Cartier, and with his fists clenched in rage, it first appeared he might rise to his feet in defiance.

Gaeten tossed in his hammock as the faces of the Iroquois haunted him—the seers had taught him to look into another person's soul for pure intention.

"I see dissension in Donnacona's tribe as he gives up his inherent fight to lead his people against those that encroach on their land. His valiant offer is not for the good of his tribe, or his sons, or even Cartier yet I am not asked to judge."

As the morning sun rose, Gaeten ventured into the thicket and sent the call of an eagle to his friend, Ruskin, hoping he was would be in range.

The sounds of the forest were alive in his ears, but he saw no signs of Ruskin. He watched for the slightest wind in the upper branches, a shadow behind a tree, or a ripple of a wave on the creek.

Instead, the hiss of a slithering rattler lured him to follow to the Iroquois lodge along a worn towpath.

From behind a giant red oak, Gaeten watched until his eyes were drawn to Donnacona's teepee, where shouting ensued between the chief and his sons.

"Domagaya, for many sunsets, we have seen the white muskets fire further than our arrows. They will continue to take our hunting grounds. There is no future here for you or your brother, as Agona is plotting to succeed."

"And you, Father—where is your future?" the elder brave challenged. "Only discord grows among our own. Agona shows his hatred toward his Chief and waits for my death. He has the taste of war on his lips ready to attack our native brothers, the Hurons, and their missions. The bloodshed of our people is not what the great spirits want."

"You are the great one, Father. Our people are indebted to you and look for your protection. Let us deceive the French into killing Agona," Domagaya replied.

"I have many years of wisdom, but you can see the ambitions of another attempting to squash me. With my sons leaving to go across the great waters, I will not have my strength."

"Do not say such words, Father. You have the leadership of your own father and grandfather before him, and our spirits too."

Enthralled by the argument, Gaeten hadn't noticed a shadow creeping behind him. Startled by a tug on his coat, he turned to see the young offen Oursin crouching beside him.

With a finger to his lips, Gaeten cautioned his friend to silence as another shape appeared from the bush, a childish, young Micmac maiden timidly watching them.

Gaeten and Oursin were paralyzed that she would betray their location. Instead, she crouched onto her knees and leaned forward with a whisper.

"You like to come with Catarina and eat?" she said.

Bowing profusely, Gaeten apologized for the intrusion and rose to leave. Looking back, he saw a smile on her face and her head tilted to watch him.

Oursin pointed toward the crew camp and gestured for Gaeten to return. Retracing their steps, neither spoke until they were safely out of range of the Iroquois.

"Why did you follow me?"

"Capitaine said that I should. Agona has a raiding party in the bush near the ship. It is not safe for you to be here now."

"Wait a moment," Gaeten whispered.

He lowered himself to listen to the soil for any vibration in the ground that would heave under their feet. He then raised his head to the wind, sniffing for the scent of the natives.

"Come now quickly!" Deftly, the pair skirted the ambush to escape back to Cartier's camp.

15

Return to Saint-Malo

In the morning, Donnacona sent a scout to the ship requesting a meeting with Cartier. When the Captain came ashore, he was met by the Chief in his full tribal dress. He carried his warrior's staff, a stuffed leather satchel, and a roll of embroidered blankets. Among his treasures was a prized, copper sword given by his village.

Standing tall, his shoulders were massive and his hips narrow with a beaded warrior's sash. Yet the expression on his broad, weathered face was telling of a great burden.

"I come too, Capitaine, to your Saint-Malo. I must see for myself that my sons are honored in our traditions."

"Agreed then, Chief Donnacona, and we will return you to your home within twelve moons."

Holding his head with pride, the aged chief marched behind Cartier not once turning to look back at his people who feared abandonment. Ten paces behind, his two sons followed with their heads down.

Feeling an affinity to the brothers being taken from their village, Gaeten befriended them as they prepared for space on the Grande Hermine.

Bowing to display his feeling of honor toward the braves, Gaeten felt the eyes of the crew on him in confusion.

"Why do you treat these people with honor?" a disgruntled prisoner on the ship charged.

"It is biblical that we are to honor all people by treating them with dignity and respect. Does the Bible not teach to love thy neighbor as thyself?"

Cartier waited, and as the braves neared, he too bowed in welcome to the Grande Hermine.

When shown to the hammocks in the hold, the brothers resisted. "Non, we sleep under stars," Domagaya stated. "We are not prisoners to be buried in the dark."

"Domagaya, you and Taignoagy will like Saint-Malo and the French people. You will learn much and be treated well by our king. Perhaps you will be taught to ride one of His Majesty's horses."

Gaeten imitated the movements of riding and watched their faces lighten to outbursts of laughter.

Taignoagy pointed to the ground. "Horse! Show me."

With a stick, Gaeten drew an image of the riding animal with a man on his back.

"Ha-ha, you ride moose," Domagaya chuckled.

Gaeten handed him the stick. "Moose! You show me moose."

"No ride moose, worse than buffalo, but good supper."

In the morning, Jalobert read aloud the list of crewmen that would remain when the ship departed.

Gaeten did not know the prisoners well with the exception of Monsieur Gobiel who had the misfortune of being a pauper. He'd been a kindly man and Gaeten was sad to see him stay behind.

Jalobert read the last name, ". . . finally, Oursin, you will stay at the Iroquois camp."

"Why poor Oursin?" Gaeten whispered in silence. "He has no skills or fortitude, he's an offen."

Finding the beleaguered Oursin shivering on the top deck huddled among drying crates, Gaeten's hand went to the amulet.

"Oursin, I have something to show you." Holding the talisman, he sat down beside his friend.

"It is expected that you might fear the unknown, but look at the opportunity to make history. When we return next spring, you will be taller, braver, and stronger in the heart. You'll know things that I never dreamed to hear. I will watch for your dreams and wishes in the stars.

"I will ask the sages to record your name in the book as a man of courage and a great explorer. I will go to your village and tell those there that you are well and a valued offen in the new world."

As Gaeten talked of the stars and the wisdom of the seers, Oursin's face relaxed as he listened.

"Merci. I am a lowly offen but you have given me hope, and I will use the powers that I have inside. Yes, you will see me next spring taller and braver. Friends forever!"

At a campfire the night before setting sail, Ruskin and Gaeten talked late in the evening as they watched the flames crackle around a wild boar roasting.

The silence told Gaeten of words unspoken, and he sensed that his friend carried a burden.

"I've decided to remain with the landing party over the winter," Ruskin said. "It is proper that Oursin should not be abandoned by his own. You said we should use our gifts to help others and my talent is physical deception, but I am also an excellent climber . . . but not too good a swimmer. When you return again, I will be your scout."

"My dear friend, my heart will be pained to leave you," Gaeten said. "I am certain you have thought about it well and hard to come to such a decision. The sages will wish you success and look forward to your return another day."

With a stick, he began doodling in the dirt to allow his feelings to permeate his thoughts.

"I would like to become a translator," Ruskin said. "I traveled to a missionary settlement inland where they have need of my skills."

"Then I leave you with your body here and I will return to Saint-Malo with memories of a good brother."

"Visit my village and tell them about my new life. When you return, bring herbs, mustard plants from Dijon, and any foreign seeds or plants that might survive the return."

In July, Gaeten sighted the harbor at Saint-Malo with Catherine and Julien standing at the pier. Instinctively, he looked to the abandoned crates for a peg-leg man.

Is that a figment of my imagination or is that Papa?

"Land ho!"

Cartier was received as the king's hero in Saint-Malo. The French flag was now firmly planted on the rocky slopes of Newfoundland, Stadacona, and Hochelaga, and soon after, each one was visited by British explorers under Henry VIII. The battle to explore and conquer the new world had become fully engaged by the Italians, Spaniards, English, and French.

While Cartier was away, others like Jean-Francois de la Roberval laid their ambitions before King Francis to assume authority for trade and explorations on the St. Lawrence.

Saint-Malo was joyous at Cartier's achievements and took a curious interest in the arrival of the native specimens of Donnacona, and his sons Domagaya, and Taignoagy.

The port had previously received pirates, slaves, gypsies and European foreigners, but never milky-brown skinned natives, with dark chocolate eyes and black, braided hair, that spoke a staccato language.

The Iroquois brothers were cynically overwhelmed at the attention and prodding. In Paris, Cartier escorted them to the royal court where they were secured in private quarters to begin their European transition.

Although, Gaeten had developed a bond with Domagaya and Taignoagy on the journey to France, the sudden separation took him off guard. Having lost Oursin and Ruskin to the native land, he felt alone and his hand searched often for the talisman for strength.

I must return to the garret at Limoilou to my sages. I have missed the curiosity and twinkle in their eyes reflecting their spirit—they will be eager to hear of my adventure.

As news of the natives in the new world encircled Europe, a movement was underway to send Jesuits to teach and convert them to Christianity and the French language.

Tales of savage deaths were glorified and the images of a hostile population were exaggerated in every alehouse. Pirates had long perpetuated tales of angry, vengeful natives in the Caribbean and it was difficult to dismiss.

Gaeten was urged to come to the tavern at nights, to tell entertaining stories of his adventure. He was now a young man with a lifetime of experience, yet the same questions echoed night after night.

"Tell us more about the natives and their barbarism. We were told they carry hatchets. Were you fearful for your life?"

The scar of the Taignoagy's spear prodding in the bush seared in his remembrance and would thrill his audience, but wisdom cautioned him.

Tell no tale that blames another. It was my doing, as it was I who was at their camp spying.

"Non. They have darker skin than a Frenchman, brown eyes, never blue, and they dress in leather from the pelts. They are wary of us. The Micmacs and Iroquois have separate personalities and build villages in a different way. They both have tribes, but each with their own character, like the French and British. As anyone would do if threatened, they want to protect themselves and their home."

"Tell us about danger," a man shouted. "We heard stories of ambushes and merciless massacres."

"The only danger was when my offen friend, Ruskin, was helping our meeting party with the Micmac. He risked his life."

Finally, there was interest in Ruskin. "Tell us about the little man. How did he risk his life?"

"The offens, dwarfs, and nymphs are ancient people, and even in Saint-Malo, they live near the bridges and hollows. They are stealthy and adept at climbing, but they look different and have the ability to camouflage themselves. Although Ruskin is the size of a young child, he is over three hundred years old."

"Don't trust those nymphs, they're thieves," a stranger called from the back of the room.

"Non, they simply collect items of curiosity and mean no harm to anyone in Saint-Malo. Shiny gadgets may disappear as they are drawn to the appearance, just as a crow would snatch something that glitters."

"I know the dwarf you talk about. He sat on the church steeple last week calculating his next attack. They think we can't see them, that they're hidden by a mysterious veil of secrecy . . ." A chorus of laughter filled the tavern, drowning out the man.

"But you are mistaken, Gaeten said. "That was not Ruskin—he is in the new world trying to be a hero for France. I am here to tell about our adventures and the courage of friends like Ruskin, the offen . . . or dwarf, as you call them. How many of you would dive into the cold Atlantic to help a friend?"

"I don't know friends fool enough to put themselves in danger on my account," another called out.

Gaeten's confidence grew as he bantered in defense.

"That's a shame, Monsieur. Is it because you don't have friends of courage? If so, I am sad for you."

With a hush, the offended man left the tavern, and eyes turned back to Gaeten to see what he would say.

"Thank you, gentlemen, for the audience tonight, but I have responsibilities to tend to. For now, all I can say is to listen well to your friends and be kind. Au revoir."

Outside the tavern, he saw the silhouette in the shadows, perched on a wooden crate.

"Bonsoir, Papa. I trust you are well." Gaeten neared him and placed a coin at his peg leg, and turned away to leave.

"Son, I am glad you have done well on your journey."

Stopping in his tracks, Gaeten contemplated returning to the man, however, he continued on his way with immediate regret in his heart.

Catherine was in her sewing room when Gaeten peered through the doorway. It struck him that she seemed older and a bit worried, but her joyous smile swept away his thoughts.

"Bonjours, Madame. It is good to be home and on French soil. I was certain that I saw your face in the brightness of the moon while we were at sea," he teased.

"Good to see you, Gaeten. The house has been much too quiet in your absence. Something about youth brings the walls alive. However, the experiments on the roof go on and remind me that I am never alone."

"The sages taught me that one is never alone—our memories are sweet comfort, and optimism for the future is our strength."

"Thank you for that truth, Gaeten. Did you enjoy being a mariner?"

Gaeten's eyes went to a beautiful leather-bound book at her side. "Is that Aesop's Fables? My mother read to me of those wonderful tales at bedtime."

"Indeed, it is a marvelous book. I was reading about the Town Mouse and the Country Mouse." Catherine laughed. "Would you like bacon and beans or cake and ale?"

"I suppose that I am a country mouse. One day I will learn to read well enough to recite the fables to my own children."

"That is not why you are here today, Gaeten. Be off to the garret, they will be waiting. We'll have our tea when you come down."

Stepping into the bedroom where he first slept at Limoilou, he looked to the wall as if he had never seen it before.

"Galileo? Copernicus? Da Vinci . . . my dear sages, are you there? I have much to tell you."

King Francis was eager for Cartier to resume his explorations to establish settlements along the St. Lawrence River. Gaeten's visits to Limoilou escalated as the Grande Hermine was refitted for its next voyage.

It was not unusual for him to remain as a house guest at the manor, and he spent more time with the elders detailing his adventure for the journals and asking for guidance.

Now a young man, he was learning to read and write under the tutelage of the elders, and he studied history, art, techniques, king's politics, feudal farming, and mechanical inventions.

Julien had taken over as livery assistant and sold from the Mansart fish mat at the market. The Hunalt's youngest daughter, Angelique, had shown an interest in Julien and there was talk of nuptials in the spring before the ships' departure.

Julien burst in to share his discovery. "Gaeten, I must talk to you. I have seen father, he has returned home."

Gaeten showed no pleasure.

"Does he want to be your Papa again or did he leave?"

"He wants to make amends, Gaeten. Can't you open your heart to an old, sick man who once gave you life?"

"My dear brother, you have grown wise and have a gentle heart. It is different with me. Papa left me alone to raise you without even a farewell. We could have starved or died and he showed no concern for us. How can I forgive him for that?"

"You think that Monsieur Cartier is your father now and you have no room in your heart for our own Papa, but he is poor and hungry. That is not right, Gaeten."

"Have I not looked after you as if I were your father? I made sure you were fed and had a place to sleep every night. Do you forget that?"

Julien's shoulders fell with exhaustion.

"Oui, mon cher frère, you have taken care of me and I'll never forget all that you have given up to provide for me. Papa has visited me many times while you were away and I'll continue to do so with or without your blessing. I love you, Gaeten."

Gaeten patted him on the back. "Our Papa made his own choice in life. He barely even knew you when he went to sea, thinking he would come back a rich man. Happiness is not measured by the amount of gold you have but the love in your heart for others. It's also the appreciation of God's heavenly constellation and the nature around us."

Silently, Gaeten walked away leaving Julien confused.

16

Awaiting a New Commission

Catherine was elated at the nuptials and insisted that Julien and Angelique wed at Limoilou in a garden ceremony. During Gaeten's absence, she had continued to visit Julien and knew the Hunalt family well.

In a brotherly conversation soon after the engagement announcement, Julien said, "Papa knows you have closed your heart to him. Madame Hunalt said you met him in the town square last year. You were kind to give him money, but you sent him on his own path."

"Look at the friends we have who care about us and what we are doing. We are rich, my dear brother."

"Oui, that is correct. Monsieur Devereau told me that if I work hard, one day the stable will be all mine. He has no sons and offered me a smithy's apprenticeship. I am learning to reshape the metal and soon will have the ability to build rims for wagon wheels, tools for farming, and even swords for war."

"Magnifique, mon frère, I am pleased to see you have found your own happiness."

From Gaeten's pocket, he handed several gold coins to Julien.

"This is from my wages at sea. I would not have been able to go without your bravery to carry on while I was gone. You are starting your own family, but we will always be the best of brothers."

Gaeten was sufficiently versed in Cartier's thoughts to answer before a question was completed. But Catherine wisely reminded him to listen until a person has said their entire story before starting his own.

"I suggest we seek out a supply of pitch made from boiled paint and tar for our ships," he declared. "I watched the Italian mariners—they say it's a strong as glue to hold repairs together when the ship is tested at sea."

"Excellent, Gaeten. Our mastership is worthy of being pampered as she has served us well. Gather some workers and tell Monsieur Jalobert what is needed for us to go deeper into the great river to build settlements."

"Yes, Monsieur. How much further?"

"Straight through to the Pacific, making a trade route to the riches of China. We will take the apothecary, Monsieur Guilbault and a priest from the Abbey to remain at Kanata. Hopefully, you will find Ruskin waiting there."

The mention of Ruskin's name brought him concerns. He wondered if the offen's appearance would be alarming to angry natives and if he would be safe.

"Excuse me, Monsieur Cartier, I have a responsibility upstairs. I will return shortly."

"Yes, I have learned not to ask, Gaeten, but it has everything to do with saving the world, I hear."

Cartier paced over to the terrace windows. He teased more, "If my wife says that it is so, then so be it."

Gaeten beamed. "So you do understand?"

"I will travel to Paris today to visit Domagaya and Taignoagy. They are receiving tutors, art classes and the finest feasts, and we have learned much about the land and what better to expect on our return. From their drawings, I know that we have many rivers to explore inland.

"Tonight I will take them to an opera and a horse and buggy ride on the Champs Élysées. The king will send escorts from his own courts."

Gaeten said. "Taignoagy especially will like that as he wanted to see a horse. It is important that the brothers learn about our culture."

Cartier placed his hand on the young man's shoulder. "We are indeed fortunate, Gaeten."

"I believe I am the luckiest. Adieu." Gaeten kicked up his heels at the door, leaving Cartier laughing.

Copernicus awaited Gaeten's arrival at the elders' chamber. "Come quickly. Leonardo is working on an invention that will interest you," he said.

On a work table, da Vinci was experimenting with a row of water goblets and held Puccini's borrowed tuning fork. The two sages worked in unity anticipating one another.

Copernicus explained, "Puccini brings the world a magical and musical soul and spent many hours in the caverns to make alterations to the acoustics."

Gaeten's wide eyes strayed to Puccini, then back to da Vinci. "It is all wonderful," Copernicus said, "and da Vinci is a miraculous man of the mind. He never sleeps at night and spends the daylight hours inventing and painting. He has accumulated a series of notes that he wants to discuss."

Puccini knelt under a board that raised and lowered with feet like a treadle. As he pressed the handles one at a time, they raised like puppets.

The pair tapped patiently on each water goblet listening for a tinkling sound to satisfy them, then repeated it down the line, altering the levels. The echoes of the glasses produced a scale of the most beautiful musical tones, and the room quietened as Puccini tapped a melody. With passion, his voice broke into lines from an opera in Italian with his eyes closed.

"Magical Messieurs, this is the music of heavenly angels," Gaeten said.

As the song ended, the goblets' chimes faded away.

"Gaeten," Puccini said, "I have something for you before you return to the new world."

From his pocket, he produced a miniature wooden flute and put it to his lips. The shrill sound carried into the caverns.

"The language of music belongs to our voices, ears, and our hearts, and the skill is in the timing. Look here, I have implanted a tiny reed that vibrates. It is the same theory as whistling through your lips."

"Like the music of the wind?" Gaeten asked.

"Precisely. Do you hear the loons calling across a lake, the clicking of a cricket on a June evening, the hooting of an owl, or the cackle of a rooster? We are all capable of noise, and thus music. Although tiny with three holes, it gives us songs with the agile fingers and the pressure of air."

As Puccini raised it to his lips, his fingers danced over the holes, filling the air with sacred and joyful music. Gaeten knew he'd remember this moment.

"You can establish a code between the ships' captains for signals as the sound carries through the air. Shipmasters could use the sound as distress signals or for messages. You try it, a short blow on a one-count, then a long blow and count to four."

With a gentle blow, Gaeten liked the reverberation, and delight lit up his face. Puccini was pleased and took four more whistles from his pockets.

"Share these with the shipmasters."

On Cartier's final visit to Donnacona's sons in Paris, he was disheartened at their declining health. Both had lost interest in extravagances and gourmet foods, and with homesickness, they longed to return to their village. Toward their own ambition, they told unbelievable tales of riches and spices, secret routes, and inland gold stashes in a campaign to secure passage back to Stadacona.

"Convince me that what you say is true. Where did the copper come from for your father's sword?" Cartier's dubious assessment asked.

The brothers looked to each other as they had been caught in a snare. "After one year of your teachings, we wish to go back. For now, send Iroquois friends, cornmeal and pemmican."

Gaeten heard about Cartier's visit and traveled himself to Paris bringing a sketchbook of pictures drawn by da Vinci of the landscape, animals, romance, and culture of the French people.

"Here in Paris, Domagaya, you can take a lovely maiden for long walks by the river under a parasol." In a pantomime, Gaeten pretended to be wearing a dress and prancing alongside.

His smile spread across his face but faded quickly as his eyes looked upward in memory and hope.

"Non, non, my dear brother. The French do not rely on the Great Spirit they seek gold and things. I long for bare feet and canoes. I have not heard the sound of an arrow in many moons."

Gaeten talked on while sketching the brothers to take back to Leonardo to illustrate their appearance.

"Adieu mes amis, keep strong in your heart."

17

Dance with the Beaver

The Grande Hermine, in full mast, led her escorts out of the bay at the end of April. The trees were in blossom and the spring gardens planted. Catherine stood on the docks with Julien when Gaeten watched from the ship and wrestled with a sensation that overcame him.

"He looks like a man, but where has my little brother gone. I should have given him more of my time. I hear old men moan like that when a child grows up and leaves home, and I am ashamed that I have that feeling. He is a married man now with his own family, and I am the one who is lost."

He climbed high to the crow's nest with Cartier on the bridge, as the shipmaster guided the helm. It occurred to him that he had grown and his fit was tighter than before.

Studying the docks, he saw old Quinntella hunched over with another of her grandsons. Hours earlier, she brought the satchel of herbs herself for Ruskin to share with the saqamaw.

Whispering, she handed him a sack, "Dear Gaeten, I am old now and fear I may not see Ruskin again. I am proud that he can teach the native Medicine Man of our secrets."

The ancient woman's hand trembled as she pushed a beaded rosary into Gaeten's hand. Not far from her sight was a disappearing vision of Copernicus.

He whispered to the wind, "Copernicus, you must seek out the old gypsy."

Closing his eyes, he imagined the kindly Copper taking the old woman by the arm and leading her away.

With Cartier's approval, the captains of the two sister ships were given whistle flutes and a signal code. Puccini watched through the telescope from the turret at Limoilou with a gleam of pride.

Once again, Cartier's fleet ran into a gale within a week of departure. Looking back through the mist, it was apparent that the Petite Hermine was lagging. When the clouds lifted enough to see a flag signal, it was agreed that its sister ship, would continue at a slower pace and rendezvous with Cartier at Newfoundland.

As the ship faded behind, Gaeten heard an emergency signal by the whistle. The ship was rapidly taking on water and the Petite Hermine turned back to assist.

Cartier decided to forge ahead, and Gaeten watched as the partner ships grew dim on the horizon. He was relieved when the rain and dark clouds abated in the following days.

Three weeks later, the Grande Hermine ran aground again on Newfoundland's cod banks and they set out the longboats to fish. Atlantic cod had become a delicacy in Paris.

The muscled crew hauled in heavy nets, with great weights of fleshy cod of at least two feet in length, still wriggling and jumping as they were hoisted above deck.

Across the bow, nets were strewn to lay and salt the fish in the June sun. Some were packed in brine barrels, and others split, salted and dry-cured after gutting.

"Bon appetite, mes amis. We'll feast tonight," Poulet declared, distributing the catch on the drying deck.

After fishing for a week, they continued on to Stadacona. Gaeten searched for Ruskin to no avail and made inquiries of any sightings of the offens.

Ruskin's impish description preceded his name, and some compared him to a creature with the agility of a small, black bear that could disappear in an instant.

Membertou said, "I spoke with your petite friend months ago at the Huron mission run by a revered Jesuit nobleman, Loyola. A man is fed by his spirit and I know Ruskin hungers for his homeland. He needs your companionship, and it is good that you have returned."

"Tell him I have a message from his grand-mère. Also, she sent these herbs for you, that Ruskin talked about."

At Hochelaga, Cartier reconvened the crew from the previous winter. The reinforcements were timely as the Iroquois and Hurons were at war over hunting grounds. But the arrival of new ships angered the Iroquois chief when the last ship limped into the bay three weeks later.

The Micmacs were intrigued by the French provisions of root vegetables, peas, and beans, and they asked for seeds and spices for the next season.

In return, they taught Cartier's crew how they farmed and grew crops of corn, squash, and tobacco. Building fires without flints, the saqamaw rolled sun-dried pine splinters between his hands until a spark emerged while women hollowed deer antlers into utensils.

Others studied Membertou's deep storage, with spruce boughs under the permafrost to prevent food spoilage.

"When the pine is not dry, take two smooth stones from the creek, and pound them until you have a fire. Preserve your campfire in the night with a cover of green ash. Remember when you are cold."

Gaeten became an artist of sorts as he drew pictorial projections of the relics used by the natives—their horticultural engineering, the structure of a wigwam, the rebirth of forests, and the spines of a canoe.

"My journals will be like navigation charts in the Book of Knowledge recording a civilization. Da Vinci will see the depths of their versatility and excel in more inventions."

Absorbed in the landscape, Gaeten found himself at a point in the woods where two creeks butted into a waterfall obstructed by a crude dam. It was occupied by an angry furry water rodent with razor-sharp teeth and a powerful tail.

Straddling the beaver lodge, he balanced on a log, fascinated by this marine beast that hadn't hibernated. As it began to roll toward him, his footing became frantic above the frigid water. With no one to help, he tried to calm himself, until a voice called out his name.

"Gaeten! Take the end of the pole."

At the risk of falling, he didn't budge but kept his stare directly on the log under his feet.

"Is that you, Ruskin? I don't see a pole, where is it?"

A branch rubbed his arm, and he maneuvered to inch toward the lifeline. Chaos was on the brink, as an angry mother beaver charged from the underwater lodge.

With a whack of her tail, the log went into a rapid dive and a spin.

"Grab it and jump on the north rock."

Gaeten's breathing slowed and he held tight to Ruskin's branch. As the log spiraled from the water, he was forced to jump. Corkscrewing into the air, the log plunged into the depths and Gaeten tumbled into the marsh and rolled to the shore.

"Were you trying to catch a beaver with your bare hands?" Ruskin jabbed in laughter.

Gaeten leaned on his elbow, still on the ground watching Ruskin. "It is good to see you, mon ami. Where have you been? You are thin and weathered. Do you regret staying?"

"For several months, I lived in a Huron mission with the Jesuits, then I was captured by Agona's Iroquois as a slave. They were taken by my appearance and treated me royally, but when they sighted Cartier's ships, they feared I would escape and they tethered me."

Ruskin rolled over in more laughing. "But we know an offen cannot be tethered."

"Will you return to France with us in the spring? Your grandmother, Quinntella, was saddened when you didn't return. She sent back herbs for the saqamaw."

Ruskin's face fell and his foot kicked at the muddy bank.

"If I do not return, tell her I am well and have the king's work here. The natives trust me, and I can ease into their camps as a translator or scout. Sometimes I'm astounded at my agility climbing a lookout tree in less than the blink of an eye."

"You must show me that," Gaeten laughed.

"You'd have liked the surprised face of a brown bear that followed me up a tree. Surely, I am the only man to outsmart the reach of the great bear's claws. See, I have started my own hero's necklace." Ruskin taunted a leather strand about his neck with an assortment of hunter's prizes.

"How has Oursin fared?"

Ruskin's face fell in despair. "He is young and has not yet overcome tragedies in life. I don't know why the sages would have sent him on the Grande Hermine."

"What happened, Ruskin?"

"He chose to remain as a slave at the Jesuit mission. It is not the life for an offen, but it was his choice. When he hears that you have returned, he will seek you out."

"Tell me about the offens in France . . . how do they fare in the caverns? Quinntella is to look at the North Star when she thinks of me. The heavens belong to all of us, and we share our souls when we commune with the stars. She will know I am there."

Gaeten drew the rosary from his pocket. "She sent this for you, Ruskin."

Holding the sacred treasure, he dabbed his face, hoping Gaeten wouldn't see the tear trickling down his cheek.

"You must be aging rapidly here with your sensitive side showing. Do you still have your powers of camouflage and deftness? I see how wise you have become in only a short time," Gaeten teased.

"I hadn't thought of aging, but you are right. Time is harder on the body here and the climate is rugged."

Instincts forewarned Ruskin of a beast surging in their direction. Fallen timber was crumbling under its weight and the spring maple branches swooned and bent. The sounds of the forest diminished as a howl sounded from nearby.

"What is it, Ruskin?"

"Shh . . . The Jesuit mission says the Iroquois have fear of a great stag elk that roams freely as king of the forest."

By then, the giant elk was upon them, with its branch-entangled antlers so wide that a path had been cleared through the bush. Snorting and heaving, the beast came to a stop, intent on a drink of water, but saw Gaeten and Ruskin between it and the creek. Its fur was matted in sweat from battle, and its aggressive pawing shook the ground.

"Ruskin, if you have any spells from Thoth, now is the time to use them. My senses cannot overcome my fear."

"Yes, you do have senses . . . listen to the animals and the winds. Imagine you have strength far greater than his."

Suddenly, Ruskin's face and body changed. With heaving and groaning, he transformed into the likeness of a glorious dinosaur serpent, the same beast that Gaeten had met in the tunnel. He rose as growls emanated from within him.

"Ruskin, is that you? What is happening?"

"I tried to deny the spell, Gaeten, but your life is in peril and I must do this . . . it is me, I am Leviathan."

Now tall, with scales of iron, the dinosaur writhed and strained, spewing fire as he stared into the eyes of the stag.

Gaeten trembled as the two beasts rose up to battle for supremacy. "I must help Ruskin. He has put his life before mine."

With rage, the stag's hooves dug in with the power of a thundering anvil, then burst forth to attack the fury of the serpent.

In a flashback, Gaeten recalled his first introduction to Levi, in the tunnel before Ruskin revealed himself. His only hope was the vision of the Ickty, the dinosaur-bird.

Uncertain but willing, Gaeten vigorously flapped his arms into an aerodynamic extension, taking flight in the form of Ickty. His adrenaline surged as his arms extended into a broad wingspan, excited by the power and force of air that was lifting him.

A raven-like 'kraa' pierced the air while an injection of fire spewed across the landing, darting and swooping.

"I will command his power while you command his spirit," Levi called as the dinosaur-bird joined him. "The strength of two is better than one."

The elk was angered but committed, pitting his life against the power of the strange beasts. He thrashed out from the trees until one of his antlers cracked. With his spirit still unbroken, he bore the anguish of his noble placement in his role to protect his breed.

Gaeten remembered words of the seers that his gift was to understand the language of the earth, the land, and the sky.

He spoke firmly. "Great majestic elk, have no fear. We are scared ourselves and we mean you no harm. If you challenge us, in fear we will defend ourselves. Native legends honor you as the Great Stag that rules the land. They pray to the spirits for protection, with almighty Wakan Tanka, the Gitchi Manitou of the nations of the new world."

The great stag remained guarded and spoke telepathically through the language of nature, groaning and moaning.

"You spewed fire on me like the natives sling arrows to bring me to my knees. My species needs me as their leader and protector—that is why I have come. You stand between my family and fresh water. The braves don't honor me, but hunt me to prove their manhood to their chief."

The serpent-dragon and dinosaur-bird felt sympathy for the stag. As their fears diminished, so did their size, until the dinosaur scales dropped and vanished into the air.

"We respect your hierarchy, Great Stag, and will not interfere with your path to drink from the creek. It was not our intention to restrict you, it was only a coincidence . . . you see the beaver . . ."

The stag pounded his hooves and heaved his bulk to the water. His head slung low and streaks of blood seeped over his crown.

"We now have a truce based on respect and understanding," Gaeten nodded.

A piercing war cry shrieked from an Iroquois hunting party having detected the great stag. From the forest, arrows fired past Gaeten and Ruskin, stinging the great oaks and maples in their paths. Gaeten recognized half a dozen eager hunters from the Iroquois village.

Ruskin shouted, "Halt! You are cowards if you attack the great stag with his back turned. Leave him in peace!"

Snickers rose from the bush. "Ah, the little dwarf from the mission. I've heard you have a spell cast upon you."

The lead brave stepped into the open with his arrow drawn, and the others followed, ready to lunge at the elk.

"All nature honors the power of its leader," he said. "You are not Iroquois and you do not understand the laws of our land."

Ruskin demanded, "Who is it among you that must obtain the legend of bringing down the Great Stag? Whoever succeeds today will dominate the others and be in line for succession. Have you determined your people's future?"

Three of the braves lowered their arrows and looked one to the other. "White man speaks the truth, the order has already been determined."

Ruskin mustered a sudden wind to bring up leaves from the ground and branches, with a blinding force.

The native leader cried out, "See, the Great Spirit is angry that you interfere."

In the commotion with the clouds of leaves and dust, Ruskin transformed into a great horned owl and flew up to perch high in the tallest red maple.

Echoing a blood-curdling cry and with fiery eyes, he spewed his rebuke. "Nature is one of the greatest spirits in the world. Leave the stag before the fire-breathing dragon returns to protect the elk."

The owl charged, diving with his talons outstretched, searching for bait. The leader of the braves remained firm in defiance and was swooped up by his hair and deposited high in the great oak.

The rest of the Iroquois scattered into the woods.

Without audible words, the owl called to Gaeten. "I must go now, my friend."

When limbs shook overhead, Gaeten knew Ruskin was gone. A shower of raindrops poured down only over him, and he thought again of the spells from the caverns.

"Truly this is a gift from the sages."

Laughter erupted when Gaeten returned to the camp drenched. "We had no rain," the shipmaster said. "Did it only fall upon you?"

Another voice mocked to his audience, "Or perhaps he had need of bathing?"

"Messieurs, I failed enticing a beaver into my trap, and the logjam overpowered me. I heard you were searching for the offen and I thought I might help."

"So where are the spoils of your hunting?" Guillaume teased, urging more hoots from crew members.

"Come with me tomorrow, Gilly. We'll bag a feeding of rabbit, wood grouse, and pheasant. It'll be supper for all. We learn from experience to challenge another to his best."

Guillaume's puffy chest calmed. "Yes, tomorrow I will go, but are you not afraid of hostile natives?"

"Why should I fear something I have not faced? Animals and warriors can smell fear, and that would put me at a great disadvantage."

As the next sun rose, Gilly stood nervously at the railing hoping the challenge would be forgotten. But Gaeten bounded up from below deck towing a rucksack, with a slingshot and hatchet looped into his belt.

"Ahoy there, mon ami, are we ready to go ashore?"

Cartier and Jalobert watched from the bridge.

"The boy has a big spirit in a small body," Cartier said.

Jalobert grunted, "I hope he knows what he's doing."

"Have you ever heard of the unseen advisers? Surely there were rumors in the des Granches household where your wife grew up." Cartier mused to himself but was overheard by Jalobert.

"Can't say that I have, Sir."

Jalobert's sextant was focused ashore on the landscape. His motion halted and he pointed to a wooded area.

"Captain, an Iroquois raiding party is to the east of the fortress. Perhaps Gaeten should reschedule his bagging outing."

"He is now a man, no longer a boy. However, ready the crew support should you hear the whistle."

18

Ambush in the Woods

By December, the Grande Hermine was encased with ice, and the crew was rationed into the shelters at Stadacona. Illness and starvation had taken at least a dozen men, and the healthy ones looked to the sky each morning for the sun and a warm breeze.

A February thaw gave hope of early spring, but by March they were closed in again by blinding snow and ice floes. The work parties went out daily for firewood and easy prey, but on this day, two did not return.

A scout ran back, bloodied and panting. "Captain Cartier, Sir. We were ambushed and unable to defend ourselves. Monsieur Gilbert was killed directly with an arrow, and Oursin was taken as a prisoner. I fear he too will not survive."

"How many?"

"I saw eight or more, and the son of Agona was among them. They were waiting for us."

Cartier and his officers reviewed the armories, set up extra watches and curtailed the shore excursions. "Batten down the hatches, men!"

The anxious crew gathered. "Winter will abate, I promise," he said. "Then we'll continue building, hauling timber from the forests at a quick pace. Spring planting will prosper at both settlements as the land has shown to be fertile. We'll reap the rewards."

"Hear, hear, Captain, we need a good harvest. I haven't seen one in two years," his nephew said.

"I have news," Cartier said. "A Huron translator has offered to lead a party to the maple bush to collect sweet water. We'll make a wooden spigot and tap into the side of grand sugar maples. As spring warms up, the sap runs through the tree's veins and out the spigot into our pails. It will boil into a sweet tasty syrup."

Gaeten's hand shot up. "Can I go with the landing party, Sir?"

Cartier laughed above the eager voices of the crew. "Yes, Gaeten, and who else do we have as volunteers?"

An Iroquois scout led the troop into the woods, moving quickly and with dexterity to clear their trail. Looking back, he saw that Jalobert's party had halted and he returned to join them again.

In the bushes, Gaeten was watching a creature high in the tree that scampered like a squirrel.

The curled toes of Ruskin. Why doesn't he reveal himself? Is danger at hand?

He listened to the sounds of the woods and the animals. Something was amiss, and he scoured the landscape.

The sky was darkening and a chilly gust gave him a shiver. The sun should have been high but was blotted out by ominous clouds that forewarned a weather change.

"Monsieur Jalobert, did the scout predict bad weather? If the sap is to run, the weather must be warm. But this sudden wind change says something different. Surely a native scout is in tune with nature."

Where is Ruskin and what was he trying to tell me?

"The morning's rain has become snowflakes," Jalobert said. "We'll build a temporary camp to wait it out. Gather spruce boughs for a lean-to—we'll move on in a few hours."

Jalobert conferred immediately with the saqamaw.

"Why do you bring us this deep in the woods if you knew there would be a storm? We could have postponed the trip."

The guide snarled, "You say you want the sweet water from the sugar maple, but not ask me to forecast the weather."

Humiliated by the tongue-lashing, the guide moved away to start a campfire. When Gaeten returned with kindling and wood, the guide had disappeared.

"He'll come back," Jalobert said. But his confidence waned as the snow was drifting high around their campfire.

"This time, we did not mark our own route," Gaeten said, "We put faith in the scout, and now our tracks are covered with snow. Monsieur, nature showed me signs of Ruskin in these woods. I will call him if you wish."

Gaeten hooted like an owl repeatedly and waited each time for a reply, as the camp crew listened in silence.

The party was ill-prepared for a winter storm, dressed in light clothing for bush work and trapping. Their tool supply had only hatchets and hammers, and only one musket.

Gaeten stood taller with his hand to his ear. "Listen, I hear the snap of a twig."

He then heard another snap closer and another. Étienne Noël lit the lantern and shone it, not on Ruskin, but on three black wolves thirty feet from them, with iridescent, hungry eyes. They stood a few feet apart, burrowing back in a fixed stare.

The crew moved closer to the fire, feeding it to an intimidating roar with any dry wood they could rummage within steps. Crackling, flaming spit distorted their vision but was keeping the wolves at bay.

Cupping his hands, Gaeten hooted again over and over, with every ounce of breath. Finally, he heard the result of his efforts in an echo.

Caw! Caw!

"Thank goodness. Ruskin is coming."

The lithe offen swung down from a tree. "Friends, why do you venture this far into the forest in poor weather?"

"The scout advised it was good for collecting maple sap," Étienne said.

"Ah, the Iroquois saqamaw? The one that left you? I fear you are being set up for an ambush. Agona, the new Iroquois chief, is displeased with Cartier's efforts at Stadacona. Are you prepared for battle?"

Jalobert's face was ashen as he counted out their meager supply of weapons.

Ruskin climbed back up the oak tree and wailed an eerie call across the sky. At the sound, the wolves scattered into the snowy woods.

A far-off, blood-curdling cry pierced the air followed by a deathly silence.

"Don't fear," Ruskin said. "My Huron friends will come to protect you. They are unhappy with Agona but they value fur trade with the Frenchmen. The river is not far, and they will come by canoe before the moon rises."

Gaeten looked to the sky but saw nothing.

"As we were taught to snare our prey, we will set our traps around the circle of our camp. If an Iroquois treads in the darkness inside the area, he will pay the consequences."

Jalobert organized the traps as the men whittled willow spears. Mostly, the effort was to preoccupy the men from imminent danger, as they were disadvantaged for battle.

As the howling of animals told of nightfall, the quiver of an Iroquois arrow across their camp set the landing party on their heels, reverberating in a stump beside Jalobert.

Ruskin called again into the night, and the cry of an owl rang back from not far away, from the direction of the river.

The Iroquois guide that had led them was now wearing war paint on his face. From the black of night, he yelped and raced with a spear aimed at Jalobert, ready for a fight to the death.

A hatchet by the fire was within Gaeten's reach. His eyes darted with furious calculation, then he grabbed for it and swiveled toward the charging Iroquois. With a force he didn't know, the weapon whirled over and over to its mark.

Two more arrows landed in the camp, the second within inches of Gaeten, before quaking into the maple carrying his red scarf.

As the Hurons mounted the slope to attack, the Iroquois retreated. Ruskin swung down from the oak and ran to the braves.

"Merci! The Iroquois will regroup and come again through the bush."

"Monsieur Many Toes, we will be ready," one of the Hurons assured Ruskin.

"Monsieur Many Toes?" Gaeten said in amusement. "Where have you been? I even searched for my cohort Levi."

"Gaeten, you do not need to rely on Ickty or Levi as you acted most courageously as yourself, as Gaeten. The great serpent is a gift of the seers and entertains battle only in dire circumstances. You were *not* at the moment of imminent death."

At the mention of the seers, Gaeten's hand went to the nautilus that was warm and revitalizing. Closing his eyes, he returned to the moment when the nautilus first swarmed him in the seers' sanctuary, mesmerizing him with its beauty and power.

Ruskin's words are a reminder that the nautilus chose to protect me yet my trust has waned. I'm like a magician with a bag of tricks that I neglected to use. Copernicus, you must know that I remember.

Agona's raiders knew they were outnumbered by the Hurons and retreated back into the woods. Then with a breeze, Ruskin was gone.

At the river, Gaeten lagged back on the path needing to commune with the sages. Facing the full moon, his eyes closed and his fists clenched, he gazed upon the North Star with his plea.

"My honored seers, my soul calls to unite with Ickty to become whole and exuberant in power. He provides more than protection, but teaches me of the extent of my inner strength."

With uncertainty, he watched the sky and recognized the great resplendent bird soaring high above him. He raised his arm as a landing site.

"Come to me, Ickty. Fly with me and see this land from the sky. What a beauty you are . . . if only you could see the strength and wonder you give me. I beckon you to permit a flight to where my friend Ruskin has returned."

Behind him, a twig cracked in the bush. His eyes burrowed into the dark soul of the deceptive scout, who was watching him and the bird.

"Cowardly saqamaw, if you speak of what you have seen, your soul will be tortured for eternity," Gaeten spewed, alarming even himself at the vengeance.

In fear, the man lowered himself to the ground.

Ickty bowed as Gaeten mounted his back. The magnificent span of his wings spread into a rainbow of feathers and aerodynamics that lifted the pair above the trees.

Clinging to the horned bird, he burrowed his head amongst the feathers until he was one being.

The dinosaur's heart beat in his own chest overcoming him with a euphoric understanding of flight and the world below. Letting go of pretenses, he allowed himself to bellow and shriek until all of his fears had been released.

Rising above the river, he watched the return of Jalobert's men stream toward the ship carrying a line of torches.

Flying north over the lush landscape with its jutting rocks and high copper boulders, Gaeten held tight over the countryside and hovered near a village of the mission's longhouses, close to the mouth of the Saguenay.

Ickty purred sensing the comfort of being close to Leviathan and Ruskin.

"Yes, dear and faithful Ickty, our friends are at hand. We come only to see that they are safe, but we cannot remain."

Swooping over the longhouses, he cawed to Ruskin who replied with a salute, then Gaeten knew that it was time to release Ickty. Silently they coasted back to the knoll where they had taken flight.

Jalobert extolled the fortitude of Gaeten to Cartier, with the tale of his heroism repeated many times that night around the campfire.

Gaeten held inside so much, but sharing his words would betray the Book of Knowledge and the works of the seers.

19

Orphan Catarina Returns

A young orphaned girl, Catarina Paraguacu, was offered as a participant from the Micmac village to provide domestic skills to Captain Cartier.

Catarina was slight with dancing, brown eyes, a broad smile, and remarkably white teeth. She took to Cartier from the beginning and begged to be taught the French language.

With care, she took her time planning her words to speak as he did. "S'il vous plaît, Papa Cartier, je parle avec ta voix?"

"My wife is Catherine," Cartier said, "and she would very much like a companion in France, as we have no sons or daughters. You could teach each other in the kitchen at the manor at Saint-Malo, a lovely town on the sea."

Cartier etched a drawing of Limoilou to demonstrate the grandeur to entice Catarina, showing its gardens, terraces, and glass windows. He spoke glowingly of the hillsides, castles, cathedrals, bridges, stone fences, cobblestone streets, fashion and a host of peculiar visions.

Her dark eyes sparked with enchanting thoughts of this French angel, Catherine, who would be waiting for her at Limoilou.

"Perhaps she could braid my hair as my own Mama used to do before she was killed. A raiding party massacred my family when I was barely able to walk. I have a few memories but I know the feeling of belonging to a family."

"My spouse longs for that feeling of belonging that you spoke of. Surely my Catherine will like to braid your hair. Will you agree to come?"

"Oui, Monsieur, I would like it very much."

When Gaeten heard the rumor of Catarina returning to France, he was intrigued. He admired her dark brown eyes and shiny black hair, but it was her gentle spirit and contentment that reminded him of Catherine.

Pour Monsieur, she is a reminder of home that I can understand yet something else is familiar.

When the Grande Hermine set sail, the last boom of the cannons sounded a farewell to the Micmac and Hurons. Catarina was at first scared, and it was Gaeten who comforted her.

Gaeten was saddened to leave Ruskin behind, but he longed for his home with memories of Saint-Malo. His appearance had changed in the two years he'd been gone. He had grown half a foot, a mariner's beard now graced his chin and a scruff of sideburns matured his look.

"I wonder about changes in Saint-Malo. Julien and Angelique likely have babies. Catherine will be waiting for Jacques and the unknown blessing of a new daughter, Catarina. Monsieur Devereau is apprenticing his new blacksmith protégé. My being, however, aches for the seers and the progress of the Book of Knowledge."

In the first week at sea, he couldn't sleep as his spirit was restless, leaving his new world adventure in anticipation of the return to France.

With growing interest, Gaeten enjoyed the presence of the Micmac maiden as she blended into the day-to-day of the ship. She was seldom idle, often pounding corn into flour meal with a wooden bowl in her lap to make flatbread, singing native ballads, or mending shirts and sewing beads for gifts to present in France.

That week, the seas became rougher, an unknown experience for Catarina. Reeling in dizziness, she leaned over the side of the rails.

She caught his eye in a different way one morning and blushed, then sagged onto the deck with exhaustion. He climbed down from the mast and went to the galley, then returned to sit beside her with a hot cup of broth.

"You are not a mariner, I see, Catarina. You must relate to the ship as if it were a hammock back in your village. Watch the clouds in the heavens and let them soothe you. Swing back and forth, back and forth. Close your eyes and let the rhythm ease you."

"Listening to you is soothing, Gaeten. But you are right, I'm not meant to be a mariner. I like steady feet and a ground to walk on."

Easing her seasickness with sips of tea, he showed her the stars overhead and told her about the wonders of Polaris. "The wondrous world is whole and round, and orchestrated by the moon and the stars."

"The moon is shining like a bright lantern, Gaeten."

"Yes, as if it is especially for us. It will follow us to Saint-Malo, the same moon that your people see. It's where we can leave messages for those we love, and you will always know that your heart is where you find a home."

Looking at Gaeten perplexed, Catarina said, "I remember you from the day you were spying on Donnacona by the red maple. You seemed determined but good so I offered you food."

Pondering on the event, it struck Gaeten of the young native girl that once came upon him and Oursin.

"Ah, oui, you were kind not to betray our presence. I should have thanked you then." He looked away with a painful thought. "Have you seen my friend Oursin since that time?"

"He was taken prisoner by the Iroquois but escaped. He was small and could disappear whenever he wanted. I heard that one of the many toes was a slave at the Jesuit school."

Sadly, Gaeten regretted abandoning his friends. "One day soon, I hope to reunite with my offen friends."

As the days wearied on, when Gaeten descended from the crow's nest, she was waiting for him. The new sensation of pleasure at seeing her confused him.

"Bonjours, Gaeten, how was the view from atop? I have missed you. Instead, I busied myself making cod stew and flat cornbread. It helps my people feel less homesick."

"You are a good mother hen, Catarina. When I was a small boy, ma mère sang lullabies to me at bedtime, just as I hear you sing ballads under the moonlight. I enjoy your telling of the Micmac spirits in the heavens and the myths of Gluscap."

"But Gluscap is not a myth, he is the father of our people."

He liked that she defended her legends defiantly.

"You must teach me more about the internal powers and relationships in nature," he said, "of the great stag, the black wolf, the rabbit, the porcupine and beaver. Did I forget any?"

She held his hand and laughed. "Yes, all of nature, even the porcupine, the fox, and the red pine."

Catarina sees the spirit and power in her people as I find in the seers and their teachings. She will be a marvelous study for the sages.

One night he found her teaching others about Polaris, pointing to the North Star. In the nights that followed, the small party of the crew and Micmacs grew as a ritual on the deck, to observe the sky and chant their worship to the heavens.

I did not expect a spiritual experience like this.

Cartier observed Gaeten's attachment to Catarina and found him alone at the railing one night, deep in thought.

"I come here too as a place to let my heart send wishes back to Catherine. It assures me that we're guided by the heavens each with a unique purpose.

"I saw Catarina's gentle spirit when you were discussing the North Star and I agree even the wonder of it brings a reward. It's magnificent to share a miracle of the stars with someone like her, not even fluent in our language. Everyone should aspire to a dream of that magnitude."

"Captain, I know now that the guides in my life are hope and destiny, and that Catarina has changed my destiny. I am grateful for this journey." Both men fell silent and gazed again at the splendor of the constellation.

Cartier sequestered himself in his quarters for most hours of the ensuing days to refine his drawings and navigation cartography.

His records logged the ship's inventories of the rafts of deerskins and beaver pelts, the barrels of salt cod, corn, hard-shelled fruits the likes of pumpkin and squash, and rock samples that he hoped would reveal diamonds and gold to please the king.

He lamented to Jalobert, "Surely this is not the passage to the East Indies, but my instincts say we found much more."

"The native scouts insist that the rocks glisten with gold and silver. We have yet to follow their inland route and see for ourselves."

"The fortresses are strong along the St. Lawrence, inland to Trois Rivières and up the Saguenay, but the sites are to be defended by the prisoner crew that the king insisted we employ," Cartier said.

"It's true that the prisoners have no fear, with nothing to lose, but only to gain their freedom. They can be bought and bartered with the natives or even the English."

"It was out of our hands once we departed. A concern is that the king now seeks a governor to rule all of New France and we will be at *his* mercy."

"You would make a fine governor, Jacques."

"Ah, but I am not in the arena in the presence of the king to submit myself, and that disadvantage will be my doom. I could not lobby for a commission as I spent time building relationships in New France with the natives. Now I'm not sure the alliances we built will hold with a new governor."

After weeks tossing on the salty sea, the crew became disgruntled and hungry. It was many days since they had sighted a distant Basque ship returning from the cod banks.

Étienne Noël braved the query of many. "Capitaine, it has been too long through the fog. Should we not have seen a horizon by now?"

"Have no fear, Master Noël. In spite of the fog and rain, we have the heavens above us. The canvases are rolled and the high poop is well engaged with the wind over the stern. We are on course and you'll soon see land to be certain."

Cartier took a flask of cognac from his pocket.

"Here lad, take a sip, it will heighten your spirits."

Noël regretted his complaint. "Merci, Sir, we will soon celebrate together in France."

In the early summer of 1536, the Grande Hermine limped into the Saint-Malo harbor and was met with fanfare and the ringing of church bells. The fleur-de-lis waved proudly from the mast, and the crew anxiously scanned the faces of the crowd, waving in the hope that a loved one waited on the docks.

The sight of the mob and the excitement of facing disembarkation was overwhelming to Catarina. She slipped her hand into the crook of Gaeten's elbow to hold tight.

Cartier's first duty on land was to take Catherine in his arms. As his weathered hands cupped her gentle face, Gaeten saw a rare, intimate expression of romance between the Cartiers.

"Catherine, my dearest, I have brought you a daughter. I adopted her. She is Catarina from the Micmac tribe."

Madame Cartier stood stunned and began to tremble. She stepped back as moisture filled her eyes, afraid to touch the beautiful, young maiden lest she might disappear as a figment.

"My dear Jacques, do you mean that I may keep her as part of our family?" Tears trickled down her cheeks.

"Yes, for now. But I caution you, she is quite fond of Gaeten and he is of her, so you might be getting more than a daughter."

She laughed freely with a joyful glee she'd withheld in his absence. Taking a step at a time, she did her best not to gush excessively or frighten the girl.

"Dearest Catarina, you are most welcome to our home."

Gaeten took Catarina's hand from his arm and nudged her toward Catherine.

"This is your new mother. I see in her eyes that she loves you already."

The household adjustments for Catarina were well-supervised by both Catherine and Gaeten, and within a few days, she ventured into the manor courtyard and gardens independently.

Gaeten was so absorbed in Catarina that in his days back, he had forgotten to seek out the thespians in the attic. With a headful of ideas and written notes to relay, he found the climb to the upper garret difficult in his mind.

Mounting the rise to Limoilou, his eye caught a glimmer of light streaming from an attic peephole. On the parapet of the window sill, with dormers opened wide, the shadow of a diminutive sage sat with a listening horn in one ear and his hand fixed on a timing scale drawn from his breast pocket.

Focusing on the window, he now saw four silhouettes, undeniably Copernicus, Galileo, Leonardo and Magellan, engrossed in an experiment of gravity. Bolstered by the apparition, he bounded up toward the garret.

Catherine grinned her approval. "They have been waiting for you, Gaeten—many hopes are planted in your reports."

"That is true. Socrates will surely guide me."

Although puzzled, Catarina made no mention of it.

Creeping into the garret this time seemed foreign and cold. The magic and beckoning that he remembered from the first occasion years before was absent.

The floorboards creaked under his weight as he neared the corner where the door had appeared before.

"Socrates, Copernicus . . . I need to speak with you," he whispered tentatively.

He heard no answer or sounds, yet he had seen the light through the attic window from the hillside.

"I have much to tell my teachers. Please, Messieurs, permit the doorknob to appear."

His heart pounded as he waited for any noise, and at last, he heard the familiar shuffle of feet.

"I beg your forgiveness, my honored seers," he said. "I have been tardy since my return. You see I have matters of the heart that I do not understand. I need your help."

Before his eyes, an apparition of the door eased into sight and the doorknob glowed dimly. With his hand on the knob, he was flooded with the same emotions he felt the first time, with a sense of wonderment and yearning.

"Come in, Gaeten. We have waited. You would have known we were on the roof to watch the Grande Hermine come into harbor last week. We were elated to see you, yet your attention was entirely on another," Copernicus said.

"What is in your heart, son?" Socrates questioned, watching Gaeten's soul wrench before them. "You have been gone two winters, and much has happened. But first, you must relieve your burdens."

"When you accepted me, I was six years younger. You see now that I have become a man, tall and muscular. But do you still see the boy in me, do I still have undeniable curiosity?"

"Oui, Gaeten, you will always be the boy we first saw, crumpled under the hoist," Copernicus said. "You were chosen, remember?"

"I hardly know where to begin, but I always had comfort searching for the North Star and I knew you would be there. My fortune was to seek knowledge and to provide that to each of my dear teachers, in return. That was my complete mission.

"Once I left Saint-Malo, my life became overwhelming. I faced solitude, near drowning, native ambushes and taking a life. I struggled to survive in the wilderness wondering if I would return to France. I was grateful that you permitted Ruskin to come with me. He saved my life more than once and I saved his."

The seers said nothing and were fixed on his words.

"Ruskin chose not to return but remained as a Huron translator at a mission with the young offen they call Oursin. Ruskin saved me from a beaver, a great stag and a deceitful scout, and on at least two occasions as Leviathan appeared and protected us."

"Leviathan protected you?" Leonardo asked. "Where were Ickty and the talisman?"

Gaeten was startled by da Vinci's challenge.

"Ickty appeared at the same time and the talisman enabled me to draw on my own inner strengths. Both were invaluable. Where should I begin? I have notes of the journey and made copies of Monsieur's cartography for the Book of Knowledge."

"You came here tonight for a reason, Gaeten," Socrates pressed. "What is that?"

"Monsieur Cartier brought back a Micmac maiden that he and Madame have adopted as their own. I have learned of her culture, legends and myths and the spirits she relies on. She came to depend on me in a way that I don't understand.

"I now return to Saint-Malo not knowing who I truly am. Julien has his own family and Ruskin is overseas. Madame Cartier has a new family now and the king's war calls to me to serve. Monsieur has no commission immediately, yet I still have the powers within me. Show me my purpose."

Socrates searched Gaeten's soul. "Dear boy, you must find your own aspiration. The world continues to turn as certain as the moon rises in the sky. Indeed you have a purpose to contribute in this world, but only you will find what that is."

Leonardo said, "Gaeten, you have appreciated the beauty in my paintings. Have you been able to show your love, joy, adventure, and more emotions? Deal with the first one before you continue in your quest."

"Yes, the first one . . . love," Gaeten repeated.

Leaving the seers, he returned to the courtyard in search of Catarina to relieve his heart. Hand-in-hand they went in search of Monsieur and Madame Cartier to seek their blessing. A simple wedding on the terrace at Limoilou was arranged for several weeks later.

Jacques Cartier proudly walked his new daughter down the garden path to where a small gathering of friends and family waited on the terrace overlooking the sea.

Gaeten invited Julien and Angelique and a one-legged man who agreed to join the party. He remained near the back, nervous yet proud, having finally achieved his own dream of regaining his sons.

20

Life in Saint-Malo

Cartier was disappointed when the king decided to postpone a return commission to the new world. The attention of Francis I had turned instead to war, ahead of exploration across the ocean.

The Renaissance Wars were involving France, Spain, the Ottoman Empire, and the Papal States, and Francis ordered 27,000 troops to invade Milan in an attempt to capture Turin. Peasants and soldiers departed from the coastal towns to join the king's forces marching from Paris.

Catarina watched the perpetual line of men leaving Saint-Malo with weapons and worried that soon Gaeten would be among them.

"Gaeten, will you need to go to battle with the soldiers from the town?"

"The time has now come, Catarina, when I must serve my king and defend France. Julien will be spared since he is charged with caring for the troop of king's horses. Monsieur Devereau has become too aged."

Catarina admired his allegiance but was pained at the imminent departure.

"Then I will wait on the hillside every evening and watch for your shadow to return to Limoilou. And every evening you are away, you will talk to me in the North Star."

During his discovery of Catarina, he had kept his pledge of secrecy to the sages. "My dear Catarina, you are among dear friends with Catherine and there are others . . . I will share my pact with you but these words must not pass your lips."

Taking her hands in his, he searched her soul as he revealed the mysteries of the sages and their remarkable guidance and insight. Taking in each word, her face broke into a smile.

"I was hoping you would tell me one day. The magnificent men believe themselves to be unseen and unheard but I have watched the changes in you when you return from the attic. I have wanted to believe something magical was held in those rafters. I am glad that you have shared this wonderful story with me."

Overwhelmed by her bravery, he regretted his responsibilities to his country over his family.

Recruited for the front lines of the king's army in Italy, his duty was not denied as he joined the overland to Turin, leaving Catarina at Limoilou.

Soon he was a valuable scout seeking out enemy hideouts, slinking into camps and listening to plans of attack. He understood the winds of conversation and tactical maneuvers but without Ruskin, he depended on the talisman for protection. Camouflaging himself and using his acquired senses, he reported back to the French commanders of the enemy plots.

In a risky predicament, he looked for a wall to seek out one of the sages. Slithering like Leviathan through the mud, he scaled up a sharp embankment to an Italian camp and shinnied up a tree. It overlooked a commander's tent by the river where the leaders commiserated with wine and fine food under the stars. Their talk grew louder as the night wore on.

"The French believe they can circle our camp and ambush us," a commander boasted with roars of laughter.

"Then we'll reinforce the night guard," another jested.

The boastful one elaborated, "Ha, ha, non, non! You see that Mario Turgeon has rounded up at least a dozen men to drop back. They have forsaken their uniforms and will disguise themselves as the French army. Once behind, they will strike suddenly and obliterate the advancement."

"When is the attack?"

"At sunrise, the fallback will begin. Our scouts are certain of where the French are sleeping."

Gaeten's heart pounded with fear about the impending slaughter. Peering into the darkness from where he came, he trudged back through the trench until he saw a glimmer of a night lantern.

Is it a French lantern or the renegades?

Enemy heads turned quickly his way and he realized he had miscalculated his retreat and was overlooking an enemy contingent. As they rushed with their bayonets closing in on him, he frantically grabbed the nautilus and held it high.

It glowed like a fiery beacon and the brightness radiated around him, blinding the enemy and forcing them to retreat in fear. He never before realized the power of the sages' gift.

Mario Turgeon boldly demanded Gaeten's surrender, but he held on tight to the nautilus with his hand trembling from the power.

"Monsieur Turgeon, you have been deceived," Gaeten said. "You are merely a decoy to your commander."

"How do you know my name?"

"I overheard your superior. You were sent as a sacrifice so your troops may advance toward safety. Surely you did not believe that you were being noble? You do not know me, but I have the power to summon a fire-breathing dinosaur to devour you and your men. Do you wish me to do that?"

Mario mocked and laughed in disbelief. "Can you not see that you are outnumbered?"

Extending the amulet above his full height like a fierce Excalibur's sword, the aura blinded those who dared look. The man's face flooded with fear and panic as his attention was diverted to the noise in the woods.

In the instant that Gaeten saw French soldiers forging in at a running pace with muskets and bayonets, he called for Ickty to aid his disappearance. A swirling rush through the bush left those on the ground dazed as the dinosaur-bird soared over the trees.

"My dear sages will be watching through the nautilus and know of my valor. I understand now.

"The power is discovery and belief in what can be changed. Thank you, my dear friends, for placing your trust in me. You have saved my life."

Returning to his camp, Gaeten told no one of his escape, but by morning word came that the enemy contingent was searching the woods for a man of his description.

One of the French soldiers described a hulk covered in mud and with an aura of power. Legendary stories spread to the enemy camps of a magical figment that fought off an entire enemy troop before disappearing like a vapor.

In the sanctuary behind the garret at Limoilou, Copernicus pounded on the great table to celebrate the victory a Turin.

Catarina was working in the garden and looked up as a troop of sages waved the fleur-dis-lis flag from the rooftop. The brief pause to this unusual vision caused time to stop for what she thought was an eternity. Galileo's gaze encompassed her and he looked into her heart and soul with a salute.

In the spring, Gaeten and other French soldiers tromped back over the hillside to Saint-Malo, his shirt torn and filthy and his boots worn through with holes. Going home to see Catarina and the Cartiers was all that was on his mind.

From the garden, Catherine was the first to see the weary soldier, barely recognizing him as he was so thin.

"He's home, Catarina . . . Jacques, come here!" She tried to contain her excitement, and tears of joy streamed down her cheeks. Catarina raced to him with her arms open.

"You've been in my dreams every night and I prayed so hard for your safety. Now we are blessed with your return."

"Bonjours, my family." His face glowed as he spoke. "You are a beautiful sight to me and I love you all."

Cartier was reserved, as his discipline. "Son, you are finally home, so rest yourself and we will celebrate with a feast. But first, a soapy bath would improve your company."

His fatherly slap on the shoulder showed his affection.

Catarina and Gaeten settled in the carriage house over the Limoilou stables. There he could attend to his chores and the studies with Cartier.

"Tell me of Turin, my love, about your battles," Caterina said. "Often I feared you would not return, but Mama assured me you will overcome all obstacles. Once, when the tears of sorrow came, a tiny man appeared and comforted me. He said the talisman would guide you home."

The tiny man . . . my dear Copernicus.

"Dear Catarina, I am never alone. This household is full of my protectors and seers that bid me wisdom just as you carry comfort and guidance from the great Glouscap."

"The spirits of the Micmac come in different forms. Glouscap is the provider and the warrior and protector of my people. He communicates with the earth, the sun, and all of nature on our behalf. I suppose he is a talisman."

Gaeten pondered the comparison in disbelief. "My dear friends of knowledge will value your legends, as mythology is a study and basis of thinking."

Catarina tightened her soft grip on his hand. Resting her head on his shoulder, she looked into the heavens.

"My Glooscap is up there beside your North Star."

Catherine prepared a family feast of welcome, with Catarina on his one side and Cartier facing him.

"Monsieur, may I ask about your next commission? Will one come soon for you?"

"Ha, ha, son, I've shown patience and had time to document my memoirs and journals. I've even perfected my cartography and remapped the coastline.

"And yes, I do have news. My third commission will be in October and will include fifty prisoners from jails across France that will live among the natives, clearing land. They'll defend our settlements and support the Carignan soldiers from hostile natives. With luck, they'll build trading partners for France too."

Gaeten said, "I've worried about our friend Chief Donnacona who is aging. I'll travel to Paris to see what more I can learn—surely he has secrets that he does not trust to the king."

Cartier nodded. "The chief has told us about the ways of his people that will help us plan colonization. He reminds us that France must respect the tenuous rivalry between the Hurons and Iroquois if we are to understand the native community. King Francis is distrustful of his motives."

"Is his health reason for concern now?"

"Yes, his health has declined," Cartier said. "Perhaps you should go right away. He values the rapport with you."

In Paris, Gaeten was ushered to a parlor where the Chief, dressed in fine cloaks, awaited his arrival. "Come in, my young friend. Sadly, you see I am frail and weaker than when I saw you last."

"We have all aged since we first met," Gaeten said. "I was a child with little knowledge. Now with an awareness of your culture, I've opened my mind to possibilities I never thought existed."

"I have learned much of your people," Donnacona said, "but I wish to return to my homeland, Gaeten. Your people want war and to take from the land for nothing more than greed. I told your king I would lead explorers past Stadacona and up the river to the gold veins in the rocks. I dream of my homeland yet I cannot empty my memories on demand."

"I will not deny you the truth, great Chief, but the king fears you are negotiating your return with an empty promise—he doubts that you found gold and the spices of the Far East. Your health is being taken from your body, and only your soul has the liberty of your thoughts."

Donnacona's head fell in submission. "When I die, I wish to be buried on the great hill over the seaway, not here in your Paris. No one is here to mourn my passing and give me a proper burial."

"I understand that, my dear Chief. One can never deny their roots and their own people, it is who we are. Although you give me the great honor of your burden, you must see that I have no power over Monsieur Cartier or our king."

With a sorrowful eye, Donnacona strolled to the open balcony. "Perhaps, Gaeten, if you are able to return to Stadacona, you will take a message back to the saqamaw for me."

"That would be my privilege. The saqamaw, Membertou, will be awaiting your return. I will convey to the Iroquois your wishes that they hold true to their traditions and beliefs. I will also tell them that you died a Christian and a great man in France."

Cartier was concerned that the news of Donnacona's death might be misunderstood when he returned to Stadacona, although his Iroquois opponent, Agona, would receive the news with pleasure.

"Gaeten, I need you to be my navigator. It's time to replace you in the crow's nest with someone younger and smaller. Set the search for a hungry, young mariner with the disease of the sea."

"You think my legs have gotten too long, Monsieur?" Gaeten chided.

"Oui and you are all of eighteen by now and have a wife of your own," Jacques winked. "Now you have other responsibilities that you must consider."

"Monsieur, how does one balance the spirit of adventure with obligations for others?"

The unexpected news came as a blow to Cartier.

"It's troubling, Catherine," Jacques explained. "My commission has run into complications, instigated by Roberval. It's postponed to January 1541."

"I'm disappointed with you. Can't you do anything?"

"It is final. De Larocque de Roberval bumped the order and demanded that *he* be prioritized by King Francis to oversee Quebec. He's been placed in charge of navigation and colonization of Quebec overruling my authority over the settlements and inland voyages. It's not my choice but I must find the patience to wait for another commission."

"I see. Father overheard the Abbott tell of Roberval's conniving with the king to obtain the appointment as Lieutenant General of Quebec."

"I fear that is so. Nonetheless, I have much to do here in Saint-Malo and I will bide my time. Explorations will never cease and I will be ready for the next commission. A plan is afoot to rid the prisons of its excess criminals and rumor suggests they will be sent to Quebec."

He paced at the terrace window, then spun around. "How goes it with our new daughter?"

Catherine whispered, "Catarina tells me that a babe will be here in the spring."

"Inevitable and most joyous. It will do the household well to have the innocence of a young child."

When the buds burst through the spring gardens, the cries of the new baby emanated from the carriage house.

"C'est un garçon! I have a son!" Gaeten shrieked.

In May 1541, the king commissioned Cartier to sail with five ships and a host of 1500 men. His brother-in-law, Mace

Jalobert, would again join him, along with Guyon des Granches and his nephews from Saint-Malo.

Gaeten struggled with the imminent departure as he had settled into family life with his infant son, Jacques, named for his godfather, and another babe on the way.

"Catarina, this conflict is painful. You know my calling is to be a mariner and go to sea with Monsieur. Julien and Angelique, Madame Hunalt, Catherine and our friends will be here, and my old Papa still watches, although he has greatly aged. If I go, teach little Jacques to watch the horizon of the Atlantic for my return."

"Yes, I will teach our children about the sea and we will watch for you in the stars. The separation will be painful, but we must fulfill our dreams. I also dream of my people and their survival. The world has invaded my homeland and now I am here in yours . . . it has become ours."

Gaeten's heart yearned for an anchor for his soul and returned to the decrepit cemetery in the church courtyard where paupers were buried. He had never spoken of this grave, yet laid a posy of wildflowers and wept. Brushing long grass from a small stone, it read in childish print, 'My dear Mama 1527'.

He had put aside the painful memory of the loss of his cherished mother. Sitting by her crude cot, he begged her not to leave this world. Then each day she weakened until she gave the last heave and squeezed his hand with all her might. Julien sat nearby sobbing but refused a sympathetic arm or to speak of his Mama again.

Murmuring a soft prayer to Louise-Therèse Mansart, Gaeten let his heart ache with longing and regret. A gentle breeze floated through the cemetery and he looked up.

"Oui, Mama, I know you are here with me. I will never forget." He leaned to kiss the broken stone.

"Adieu."

Approaching the day of departure, Gaeten found solace with the seers. His spirits were heartened at the burst of new inventions in the caverns and the volumes of energy written in the journals.

The colors of Leonardo were more brilliant than ever and stirred a depth of vision that he had forgotten.

"You see, Gaeten, we will go on without you," Copernicus said. "But words we have given you from the beginning remain true, and you have the same soul, with greater strengths and resources."

The wise old man pointed his finger in Gaeten's face. "Always remember those who have been kind to you."

Gaeten flashed to Ruskin, left in the new world to find his own way.

"Did you see the old woman . . . Quinntella?"

"Oui, the ancient one," Socrates said. "She visits and sits by the journals many days to recount her stories and the legends of her people. Her insights are remarkable and her vision of Ruskin's contribution to the world is profound."

"Did she leave a message for Ruskin?"

Copernicus and Socrates exchanged glances.

"Dear boy, even nymphs do not live forever. Her strength has departed, yet her soul is strong. Her only wish is to see Ruskin once more. We do not know the answer."

"I will tell Ruskin of his grand-mère, but a man's heart belongs only to himself. If Quinntella wishes him to return, that may not be what is best for Ruskin."

"Ah-ha! I see you have acquired wisdom of life," Socrates cackled. "We cannot make decisions for another."

Overwhelmed with a sudden emptiness, Gaeten wrung his cap in his hands and bowed before the seers.

"My wish is to see all of you soon. As my body goes again, my heart remains here with Catarina and little Jacques . . . and my dear teachers."

"Oui, little Jacques…we have great aspirations for him if he is like his father."

Galileo winked.

21

Third Commission Fails

As weapons and tools were rounded up and stored in the armory, the navigation crew labored over the statistics of provisions needed for trading. Strategies and regulations for such a large contingent meant rigorous study, and Cartier insisted that a military unit be assigned to provide order to prevent improbable mutiny.

Reports from Roberval indicated native uprisings led by Agona at Stadacona. The Iroquois resisted the explorers and fur traders, resorting to ambushes and massacres.

The great nations divided their loyalties, the Iroquois to the English and the Hurons, Algonquin and Micmacs to the French.

Cartier pondered an option.

Perhaps the saqamaw, Membertou, will align with us. We need a loyal guide to take us inland to the gold that Donnacona tells us about.

Building more fortresses along the St. Lawrence would be essential for the habitants' survival, and Cartier chose a new site he named Charlesbourg-Royale at the mouth of Rivière Cap de-Rouge, with an abundance of white cedar.

The expedition across the Atlantic was without incident, with prisoners chained together on the second and third ships for oar manpower when the winds were low.

A boy from Poitou named Augustine was appointed to the crow's nest of the Grande Hermine. Taking the lad under his wing, Gaeten's intent was not to strike fear into him but to establish a sense of obligation.

"Augustine, you have a vital responsibility as the eyes of the captain. Be on your guard whenever you sit here in the basket."

"Oui, Monsieur Mansart, I will not disappoint."

"Was your father a mariner?"

"Non, but I taste the sea salt on my tongue every day and I dream of my privilege to serve on an exploration."

Gaeten tousled Augustine's hair as he remembered Cartier doing to him on his first voyage.

Entering the seaway after three weeks at sea, the water glittered like diamonds below the high, red cliffs. The beauty of the landscape awed him as if it were his first sighting. Searching the shore, he hoped to see the Micmac.

"Dear saqamaw or Ruskin, I wish you to appear."

He meditated with his hand on the amulet, knowing that it was for protection, not for his own wishes.

As the crew labored to build the new fortress, Gaeten assisted Cartier with his duties and joined the morning scouts in searches for game and water. He knew to allow for mistrust of the Iroquois natives.

On an early morning duty hiking for game, the native scout abruptly raised his hand.

Gaeten stood in silence to wait, and in those moments he focused on his senses. Looking over the treetops, he saw a flight of birds, not swallows or sparrows, but hawks circling over a rise.

With hand signals, he advised the scout that a hunt of nature had taken place and they should not intercept an angry beast. But it was too late.

A great roar blasted through the bushes, and standing on her hind haunches was an enormous, brown mother grizzly. Her cubs were feasting on bush berries nearby.

"Don't interfere with the circle of life," Gaeten cautioned, "Step back slowly, do not run."

A French prisoner did not fathom the warning and turned on his heels to retreat, a fatal mistake. The she-bear raged at him at full speed, with her fangs and claws as her only defense to protect her cubs. The shrieking was terrifying as the victim was taken in the jaws of the grizzly, tossed and dragged to the bushes.

"Slowly retreat, we cannot save him now," the scout commanded. "Drop the spoils of our hunt and leave it here."

The beleaguered troop returned to the fortress shaken.

"What has happened?" Augustine inquired.

"Someday there will be a story to tell," Gaeten said, "but grief cannot be put into words. My wife is a Micmac and told me tales of the ferociousness of this Great Bear and now I have seen it for myself. Yet I know of another beast, a Great Bird that soars above the forest."

After several months, Cartier was called to meet with his nemesis Roberval at Stadacona. The inroads that Cartier made with the Micmacs and Hurons had aggravated the new commander, and he did his best to stifle Jacques' spirit.

"We are not in agreement on how the settlements should flourish, Captain Cartier. The Iroquois must be squashed and not squander either our trading rights or the land staked for our king. We are a superior people and do not negotiate with these tribes."

"With respect, Monsieur Larocque de Roberval, the king ordered settlements along the St. Lawrence. If we cannot live in harmony with the native peoples, there is no hope for survival. It is a vast land with room for all—the indigenous tribes, the French and the British. If it is only a matter of which flag flies, it is a sad time."

Over several days, the debates continued as resentment grew between the two men until Roberval came to an irreversible decision.

"Captain Cartier, you will return to Saint-Malo as soon as the waterway opens again. Your leadership has been appreciated but is no longer necessary. I have a new vision for this new world and you are not to be part of it."

Dumbfounded, Cartier returned to the Grande Hermine and his cabin. When he did not appear on deck for two days, Gaeten was concerned and went to his cabin.

"Captain, Papa, I wish to speak with you."

"It is open, Gaeten."

"Word has come from the scouts of your meeting. It is with great sadness that we return, but it is the will of God."

"The will of God? Non, the will of Roberval. Not even the king knows of the truth of these people and this land." Cartier poured himself another brandy and raised it to his lips. "To the King."

In the spring of 1542, Cartier's entire contingent returned to Saint-Malo where he was temporarily stripped of consideration for future commissions. Roberval had poisoned his report to the king and not even the Abbott or Monsieur des Granches could intervene.

Cartier was appointed as one of the king's chosen cartographers to maintain royal navigation charts for French explorations. This disguised honor required extended absences from Saint-Malo to attend the royal court in Paris.

Gaeten bore the disappointment of the return of the expedition, but in the winter, he delighted in his family as Catarina gave birth to a daughter at Limoilou. When not on the battlefield, he worked in the vineyards and livery stables.

Rarely did he go to the attic or call for the seers, and the doorknob had not appeared in some time. Yet every day, he carried the amulet deep in his pocket as a reminder.

Tragedy struck as Europe succumbed to the ravages of the black plague, and Saint-Malo was not spared. Returning from Madame Hunalt's funeral, Gaeten found Catarina lying in the garden with wee Charlotte crying at her side.

"What has happened to Mama?"

"She is sick, Papa, very sick."

"Where is little Jacques?" Gaeten asked as he bent over Catarina.

Charlotte pointed to the carriage house. "He is too sick to get up."

"And Madame Cartier?"

"Her father needed her. They left with the carriage this morning."

Catarina was limp and burning with fever when Gaeten laid her on their bed. Little Jacques barely whimpered but was fraught with sweat.

"Charlotte, you must not come near. This sickness is contagious."

The night was long, tending to Catarina and Jacques, but it was the young boy that showed the only improvement by morning.

"Papa? Mama is dying isn't she?" Jacques asked.

"She will not die. We need Mama, she cannot leave us."

As the day darkened, the sounds of the carriage coming into the courtyard were a relief to Gaeten.

Charlotte bounded to the window. "It is grand-mère et grand-père." She scurried out to the carriage with the news, and Catherine rushed back with her.

"Gaeten, what can be done? The doctor will not come as too many are sick in town."

"Jacques is doing better and perhaps some broth will give him strength. I will not leave Catarina."

Dabbing cloths of cool water on her brow, he was flooded with her spirit. He could not bear to be without her love.

"Dearest," he whispered, "let me tell you a Micmac tale of fortitude and survival. You must listen and find your will to survive."

He placed the talisman in her limp hand and folded her fingers around it. "Believe that you are protected, you must live, my Catarina."

Her eyelids fluttered and the faintest expression crossed her face, her gentlest smile. "Mon dear Gaeten, I must go to my mother now. Guard the children well and make sure your talisman is Jacques' beacon."

Her fingers unfolded and the light of her soul went away.

Gaeten's despair was insurmountable, and Catherine and Jacques feared for him as they found him day after day in the garden sobbing on his knees.

Catherine touched his shoulder. "Remember when you first came to Limoilou, it was the seers that gave you light. Perhaps it is time to seek them again."

"I have gone to the attic, and they do not come. There is no answer and no doorknob. They must know about my anguish and see my desperation."

"Perhaps it's time that you need with your grief. You must remember that you have two small ones that need their Papa. It is for them that you will strengthen and recover."

"Oui, Catherine." He rose from his knees. "Today I will walk down by the old gypsy village."

"Take the luxury of time, and I will tend to Jacques and Charlotte."

From the entrance she watched Gaeten saunter toward town, carrying a heavy heart.

22

Where Have They Gone?

The cathedral bells of Saint-Vincent-de-Saragoose peeled at 11 a.m., the moment Gaeten passed the livery. Julien was occupied, mounting a wagon wheel, and didn't notice the thin, beleaguered man passing.

The Hunalt's shop was still shrouded in a black curtain as the family mourned the loss of their matriarch. Nearby, other shops were boarded and vacant as a funeral procession moved into the cemetery.

Gaeten followed it halfway, then veered toward an ancient yew tree in the far corner. Bent over, his hands brushed away the tall grass for the cool, rough footstone.

"Mama, I cannot bear to be a father to my little ones without Catarina. Tell me what to do."

Memories flooded to him of sitting on his mother's lap. Her soft reassuring voice was telling him all would be well in the world if he only believed. She always told him he would be loved for eternity.

Her words repeated in his thoughts. "Remember, sweet Gaeten, my spirit is with you whenever you look upon the stars."

"That is how it all started—with my mother. My hope, my world, and my future are all in the stars."

He stood up with renewed determination.

Rushing to get to the gypsy village by the bridge, he skipped past the briar bushes, anticipating his reunion with the offens. As he ran, clouds darkened the sun with an ominous sensation.

"Mon Dieu, what has happened?"

Where the offen camp had been, he saw nothing but overgrown ruins, weeds, and a graveyard with crumbling stones. Not a soul was in sight and the river he knew had no current, not even a ripple.

At the graveyard, he stopped at a recent mound of soil with a white cross. In disbelief, he rubbed his eyes at the words. 'Quinntella – the eyes of wisdom'.

"How much grief am I to bear this day?"

He knelt with his hand on the cross and wept. Laying a blade of sweetgrass at its foot, he said, "Every stalk of grass has been a part of this world and will not be forgotten. Thank you for giving me Ruskin."

Standing in the night, he looked for the stars to twinkle in heaven and leave him solace. In the darkness he found his way to the river, searching against the sky for the outline of Limoilou, and hoping to see the cast of seers on the roofline.

On a rock by the river, he drew the amulet from his pocket, closed his eyes and reflected on his adventure with the seers.

"In my earliest encounters, when the seers talked of the betrayal of Clovis, they said he escaped the cavern from an unknown portal. How can I find that without the help of an offen? Surely I can redeem myself."

In the morning, Gaeten left the children with Catherine and hiked up into the countryside in search of the secret entrance. Stumbling over rocks and sliding on muddy inclines, he pushed onward in his determination to succeed.

The pathways were overgrown, yet he searched for the smallest clue. On a hill parallel to Limoilou, he stooped to the ground finding a scrap of Persian silk with a golden thread the color of a serpent. Nearby were remnants of pearly blue scales and iridescent feathers.

"I should not fear the curse of Thoth, as it is only something I have heard and never felt. Aristotle encouraged me not to fear the unknown, as it is a loss of adventure and prevents achievement."

Ahead on a rocky slope, Gaeten saw the image of an offen and watched it scramble into the bushes. Looking upward, he imagined the great bird Ickty flying low over the lavender fields, then bounding after the serpent Leviathan.

Jumping on his toes, he waved and shouted, "Ahoy, my friends. Dear offen, I come in friendship."

On his knees, he patted the soil, hoping for a sign of the wayward offen, then he crawled to the location. A startling vision of a brilliant red berry bush was wedged into the side of a rockface.

"I have never seen such vegetation. I can't be dreaming."

At the shrub was a gap in a rock that was large enough for an offen, but not for Gaeten. Struggling, he tried to squeeze through, but it was in vain.

"I will tell the seers what I found. Surely they will be pleased."

Returning along the sea's rocky shore to Limoilou, he descended to watch children collecting barnacles and clams.

He recalled his boyhood days, then vivid memories of the seers, of Ruskin over in the new world, the dinosaur serpent Leviathan and the kindly bird Ickty. He was grateful for the voyages and adventures as Cartier's protégé. But mostly for dear Catarina.

"Where have they gone? They were each part of me and enabled me to become myself."

Looking out at the ocean he felt calm and reassured.

"I have never spoken to another mortal of the powers of Levi, Ickty, Ruskin, Copernicus, Galileo, Aristotle, Socrates, Magellan, Leonardo, Puccino and the other seers. My secrets died with Catarina. If I cannot share my powers and my memories, what is left?"

The talisman warmed in his pocket. "Ah yes, you are proof. You hold the door to my past, my spirit, and my hopes. I have believed in myself and have overcome the impossible. I am a man without these apparitions."

He coddled the amulet as it glowed in iridescent colors.

The sun was setting on the sea with the outline of a galleon on the horizon. Movement on the slope drew his gaze . . . the likeness of an offen that looked like Ruskin. A roar from behind sounded like the playful Levi frolicking after Ickty as they chased crabs.

Up at the terrace, the seers were there once more. With the talisman to his lips, he smiled with a joyous heart.

Catherine was heartened to see Gaeten sprinting up the laneway and little Jacques running to his open arms.

"Merci, Mama Cartier, you are an angel."

Gaeten kissed Catherine's cheek, then the top of Charlotte's head as she stretched her arms to him.

He was fully aware this was the first time he had referred to her as Mama. She slipped her arm across his back as the foursome returned to the garden.

Charlotte raised a handful of wildflowers. "We have been picking flowers with Grand-mère for Mama's grave. She will be expecting us, Papa."

"Oui, ma cheri, we'll go to talk to Mama, and then I will take you to the ocean and show you where I used to play. I have many stories to tell you."

"I love the adventures of your stories," Jacques said. "Mama told us Micmac legends every night."

"Wait, Gaeten," Catherine said, "I will prepare a beach picnic. The fresh air will be right for all of you."

On his boyhood footpath, Gaeten eased the children over his rocky slope and chased them in the sand. With his hands, Jacques dug for clams and shells and eagerly bagged crustaceans for Grand-mère.

Monsieur Gallipeau no longer drew his lobster traps, but others had taken his place. It was a good day for fishing, for children, and for a dad, a day to laugh and smile.

"I have some adventures to tell you today, my dear little ones."

"Ah, oui." Charlotte clapped her hands in anticipation.

"There was once a boy a bit older than Jacques is now. Like you, he lost his dear Mama. When he was sad he looked inside himself for strength to find goodness in the world."

Jacques was confused. "I can't see inside my heart, Papa. What do I do?"

"It is for you to find out—that is the great puzzle in life. The boy I am telling you about lived here in Saint-Malo and had many kind people to look after him. Living at Limoilou, you can both see across the ocean to imagine a new world far away. That boy longed to go on one of those ships for adventure to see what was on the other side."

Charlotte's face tightened with worry. "But he would have to leave his family to go so far away. That would be sad for them."

Gaeten nodded at her innocence and wisdom.

"You know when Mama went away . . . she didn't leave us, as she is in our hearts and our memories. Wherever you go, she will follow. Mama will always gently kiss your foreheads goodnight and watch over you from the heavens."

Jacques looked out to sea in quiet thought.

"You will not leave us, will you, Papa? I heard Grand-mère and Uncle Julien talk about when your own Papa went to become a pirate and never returned. Please don't become a pirate."

"You have a wise heart, son. I promise not to leave you as my duty is here at Limoilou to be your father and protect you. I will become your seer. Once I had secret friends that gave me good advice and taught me well in the world. Later I realized that what I thought they had given me, I had inside all the time."

"What did you have inside?" Jacques asked.

Taking the talisman from his pocket, he fondled it in his hand until it warmed and became beautiful.

"In my hand, I hold only a symbol. In my heart, I have faith, hope, courage, love, and a desire for knowledge. My quest can be achieved only as long as I depend on my own gifts and powers."

Gaeten put his face beside Jacques and pointed to the roofline of Limoilou.

"See up on the roof, if you look closely you will see three men sitting on a board. Look long and hard."

Squinting and trying his best, Jacques saw nothing.

"You have to believe in your heart that they are there, Jacques. Try again."

The talisman was shining brilliantly. "Ooh, Papa, it is so pretty," Charlotte said.

Still watching the roofline, Jacques turned. "Papa, I think that I see them. One is waving a kite."

Gaeten was aghast and his head swung around.

Looking back at the sea, Charlotte announced, "Papa, a great ship is at the harbor with a fleur-de-lis and giant white sails. A funny man is on the bow waving to us."

"I can't see him, Charlotte. What does he look like?"

"He's like the offen you told in the beaver story. I'm sure of it. The one that climbs with many toes and dresses like a child. I want to believe it is Ruskin, returning to his village. They must have missed him awfully."

"Ah, yes, he was the friend I needed and my rescuer when I failed myself. He never gave up on me."

"He looks so funny. Will you tell us another story about him?"

"Better than that, I'll take you to the offen village where Uncle Julien and I escaped on Magellan's raft."

Knowing the abandoned camp was barren, Gaeten refused to give up on his dreams.

"Can I ride on your shoulders?" Charlotte pleaded.

With Jacques in hand, the trio hopped and skipped down the pathway to the bridge. Gaeten could not believe his eyes.

Ahead was a wisp of smoke from a campfire, with singing and dancing by a strange group of nymphs and dwarfs. The ruins had been resurrected and revitalized, and in the midst of the dance circle was his beloved Ruskin.

Gaeten rushed to hug the man. "Ahoy, matey."

"My dear friend, Gaeten, I was about to seek you out but first I had to find my people. Our ship has returned and I came directly to the village."

Ruskin's eyes fell upon the two little ones.

"Ah, this is Charlotte with her mother's smiling eyes and Jacques with his father's blond curly hair. Gentle indeed."

The children giggled as they inspected the oddities of the offens. Each, in turn, came close to peer into their eyes grunting with pleasure.

Embracing his offen brother, Gaeten looked over at the camp. Sitting on a rock was old Quinntella, weaving a bulrush basket. When she spied him, she hobbled with a willow shillelagh walking stick toward Gaeten and Ruskin.

"We are glad to see you, Gaeten. I received the sad news of Catarina and I send our sympathies. So many homes are boarded up and visitation is prohibited."

"The children and I are well, Quinntella. But how have you fared?"

"Now that Ruskin has come home, all is well again."

Gaeten reached to touch Ruskin's elbow.

"I needed to know that you are real."

"Old woman, my Mama told me stories of Gluscap from the land where your grandson has returned," Jacques asked. "Did you know my mother was an Abenaki Micmac? It is hard to say without practice. She told me stories about kind dwarfs that look like you—they hide and seek in the forest."

Laughing she took his chin in the palm of her hand.

"You are a delight, young man. I would love to hear your Mama's tales. My Ruskin has told me of the Micmac people who taught him their ways."

As Charlotte fell asleep, Gaeten told stories of the Micmacs to the fascination of the offens gathered around the fire.

23

Dinosaur Legends

The next day, the children begged Gaeten to return to the ocean for more tales of adventures and to bring back mussels for their Grand-mère.

"The sun is barely in the sky. I must do my chores first, then we will go. I promise."

With the horses groomed and pastured, Gaeten silently slipped up the back stairs of the manor to the attic.

"Dear seers, I have come in need to relieve my spirit and tell you what I have learned. I know you are curious. Please open the door."

With his ear to the wall, he heard soft, distant humming from the caverns and a conglomeration of animal noises. Then he heard an arthritic gait, and the doorknob glowed.

"Bonjours, Monsieur da Vinci, I am glad you are looking well."

"Looking well, you say? I'd never thought of myself that way, and indeed I have done a portrait or two of my own face. I hope you see wisdom and creativity and not ill health."

"Ah, Monsieur, it is how townsfolk talk and means nothing. You always are magnificent and inspiring."

"I was saddened to hear of Catarina's passing, Gaeten. Her spirit was unique and I valued the Micmac tales she told to the little ones. She was blessed with more life than many, but with a willingness to let her spirit seek."

"That is right, and we miss her terribly. I will take the children to the graveyard today if the church allows it."

Behind him, the background had filled with curious seers and friendly faces.

"Yesterday was a day of unleashing for me and I wanted to tell my closest friends of the joy I have found."

Copernicus dabbed at a teary eye at his words.

"Through my own children and my searching, I have come to understand so much of what you intended to teach me," Gaeten said. "I have great respect for your works in preserving knowledge, but I realize the powers you talked about to me were inside me all along.

"The deference and transformations in the likes of Leviathan and Ickty made it easier to comprehend, but I know now that Leviathan is the incarnation of Ruskin and Ickty of myself. Their friendship and protection gave me fierceness and courage."

Socrates rubbed his chin with amusement.

"Is that so? You do not mean to tell us that the ancient dinosaur and serpent do *not* dwell in the caverns."

"Certainly they do and I will fondly remember them there. I was desperate to get into the caverns yesterday to reassure myself of its existence and I found Clovis's concealed entrance. Unfortunately, I have grown too much to squeeze through, but someday if you need a little boy, my Jacques will take the task equally."

He had so much to say but time was short when he heard little Charlotte calling from the yard below.

"Papa, where are you? We are waiting to go to the beach."

"Bless you, my dear friends, we are one."

Frolicking on the beach, the children filled their catch basket, then Jacques tugged at Gaeten's shirt sleeve.

"Papa, tell us about Levi and Ickty."

"Little Jacques, there is a secret chamber below the hillside not far from Limoilou, where an ancient serpent-like dinosaur lived alone as his species was extinct. The first people to encounter him were frightened and called him devilish names such as Leviathan. He was meant to be a fire-breathing dinosaur of great power, but in fear, he slithered away like a serpent finding comfort in a rock crevice.

"One day a boy entered the dark and lonely cavern. He too was frightened, but the fear inside beaconed for a prehistoric dinosaur-bird called Ickty to appear, with power to ward off his fears.

"They stared at each another and miraculously bonded, with Ickty accepting the outreach of the boy. Hearing the joyous meeting, Leviathan, the ancient serpent-dinosaur puffed himself with strength and courage and found his way through the tunnels to the bird and the boy. The reunion between Leviathan and Ickty was wondrous."

"I'd like to go there and visit Levi and Ickty, Papa," Jacques said. "They could come to the seashore, or play fetch with us. Mama told us how Gluscap can call upon the water mermaids to play. We could all be friends."

Gaeten grinned and held the amulet with both hands. Closing his eyes, he wished to see Levi and Ickty through the imagination of a child, frolicking on the beach with the mermaids and with the seers overlooking.

The sun warmed his face and he felt alone until Charlotte touched his cheek.

"Did you hear that Papa?"

A cry and a roar mounted the rocky slope. High on the crest was the great Ickty, flapping in full wingspan and calling to Leviathan as he bounded across the knoll. The excitement and reunion of the two ancient dinosaurs flooded Gaeten's eyes with tears.

He opened Jacques' hand and folded the boy's fingers around the amulet.

"This is for you, son. Use it with Charlotte and you will find all the adventure and imagination the world has to offer. It will also keep you close to your memories of Mama."

"Ooh, it is so beautiful," Charlotte cooed, stretching to touch it.

Jacques closed his hand on it and raised it tight to his heart. "Papa, we will cherish this."

"It is magical, Jacques, and will bring great men to visit you, teaching of wisdom and their inventions."

The children talked on with excitement, and Gaeten silently recalled his first visit to the thespians, with visions of the animals, the whirring of mechanics and floating images of inventions—the awe and wonder of the unseen and unknown, all parts of the Book of Knowledge.

The eager faces of Copernicus, Galileo, da Vinci, Puccini, Aristotle, and Magellan flashed before him, the transitional seers that guided him through his journeys.

He struggled for the words of his earliest meeting with them.

"Leonardo told me, 'First, you must believe in yourself. Think long and hard on that. Each person has powerful qualities and resources. Don't look for the tangible, but for the unseen.' The seers said, 'Undeniable curiosity is the key to the universe—the door to wisdom and knowledge and a true understanding of the world.' "

Life as a mariner was Gaeten's test in learning, but was behind him now, as life returned to normal in Saint-Malo. Surrounded by family, he toiled in the vineyards, and from time to time he looked up at the roofline of Limoilou and wondered.

One afternoon, he saw the peg-legged man entering the cemetery behind the church. Following, he found the old man stooped over the grass-covered stone in the corner. A shudder came over Gaeten as he crept closer.

Laying his hand on the man's shoulder, a surge of anguish flooded his soul while the stooped gent knelt at the broken stone.

"I hope I am not too late, Papa."

As the next years passed, Gaeten sat regularly on the hillside with his failing father, often watching Jacques and Charlotte play on the beach chasing the paper dragon kites that Galileo had made.

"I never asked, Father, where you went and how life has been for you. I regret not sharing with you my adventures and the insight in life that may have given you a dream."

"Dear Gaeten, all my dreams have come true. I am here with my son and my grandchildren. What more can an old man want?"

"Father, I have many tales to tell you, then I would like you to accompany me and Jacques to the red bush. There you will see the many secrets of the past and present to be revealed."

"A red bush? I don't understand, but I will follow you wherever you wish me to go."

Old Mansart gave of his heart but then his smile faded as he looked down upon the wooden peg.

"Perhaps I am not as able as you think, Gaeten."

"We won't know then, Papa, until we try. To me you are whole, but I had forgotten of your misfortune. Let it be so tomorrow, but first I need permission from my teachers."

"Ha, ha, you are much too old for schooling, Gaeten."

"Non, Papa, we are never too old for schooling."

It was early in April, at a time when ships were sailing across the Atlantic from Saint-Malo. Still as ever, throngs of sailors, merchants and townsfolk gathered at the pier to bid adieu. Old Mansart hired a donkey cart to take him up the rugged road to Limoilou to meet Gaeten and Jacques.

Meanwhile, Gaeten had gone to seek out the seers. Copernicus was filled with anticipation at the prospect of young Jacques breaching the tunnel from Clovis's hidden entrance. In the air, he waved his hand to bring the others for a conference.

Galileo tucked his thumb into his pocket and stretched like a proud peacock.

"Oui, Gaeten, we will be anxious to see young Jacques' success. He is just as his father was when we first chose him.

"Does the boy know of us?" da Vinci asked with anxiety and excitement?

Gaeten was amused by the invigoration of the seers at the prospect of another protégé in the young boy.

"Jacques has heard bedtime stories since he was a baby, tales of Glouscap and Aesop . . . and of offens and seers. He has become a believer in wonder if that is what you wish to know. But with respect to each of you as my teachers, I have never taken him to the sacred doorknob."

Copper sighed with satisfaction. "I see . . . but you do agree he has the spirit of curiosity?"

Gaeten nodded. "He has no less than my own."

He pulled a piece of burlap from his pocket and unfolded the fabric, revealing the tapestry threads from the hillside, and showed the seers the green scales he believed belonged to the serpent-dragon.

"I found this on a distant hill, where I was drawn to a crimson burning bush wedged into a rock. That is where I recovered these clues."

Galileo's bony fingers reached for the evidence. "Please, may I have a closer look?"

Copernicus repeated, "A crimson bush?"

"Gentlemen, it's remarkable," da Vinci declared. "On many nights I've had a vision of such a location. This is a message being revealed to us. Wait here, Gaeten, I have something for you to see."

Leonardo scurried into the cavern and Gaeten's gaze followed. The aged artist rummaged through his sketches and seized a small sketchbook. Returning, he produced a colored picture of the red bush wedged into the rocks."

Gaeten was astounded. "Remarkable, Monsieur da Vinci, it is as you have portrayed."

Galileo proposed, "I will send for Ruskin. He is still lithe enough to go into the tunnels. At least there will be another to provide assistance should Jacques lose his way."

"Oui, to get Ruskin—that is good."

"Time is wasting away," Copernicus affirmed. "We are now in reach of this notable landmark in our journey, and our anticipation is unabated. Gaeten, are you prepared to proceed immediately?"

"Now, you mean?"

"Yes, right away! Never put off what can be done in the moment." Leonardo said, clapping his hands.

"Jacques awaits me in the garden. My Papa wishes to be part of the adventure, but he is physically not able to make the journey and must stay here at Limoilou with Charlotte."

Da Vinci admonished him with kindness. "Non, Gaeten, do not see him as a hindrance, but let him find his inner strength and go as far as he can. There is never shame in trying our best—his only limitation is what you imagine or he agrees."

"Monsieur, I am ashamed for making a conclusion on behalf of another's ability. Yes, I will encourage him and slow my pace to his."

Descending through the summer kitchen, Gaeten heard laughter in the garden, of Madame Cartier in a rocker, teaching Charlotte and Jacques rhymes. Old Mansart sat in another with a twinkle in his eye, the first time Gaeten had seen a smile on his face.

"Merci, Madame, for entertaining my family. The seers have given consent that we begin our adventure today."

Jacques' eyes were wild. "Papa, can I go into the magical caverns? Have the wise seers given me their trust?"

"Oui, Jacques, it will be."

Catherine winced. "Someday, perhaps, you will take me along as well. But this morning, Charlotte and I will plan a special day and we start with braiding her hair like her mother's."

With a sturdy burrow from the corral, Gaeten hitched a cart with a cushion for old Mansart, and beside him, he packed supplies, hemp ropes, lanterns, canteens and a pair of shovels.

Charlotte ran alongside until they reached the upward path. "You will look back and wave to me, won't you, Papa."

"Indeed, I'll be looking for my dear daughter. I always look back to see who is behind me."

His words echoed to the moment when he turned back to see Catarina on her knees at Donnacona's camp.

The terrain was rugged and tedious with the cart but with optimism, the trio forged ahead. From time to time, Gaeten recalculated the distance through the sextant.

"Here, Old Papa, the crimson bush is about a half-hour uphill. I fear we cannot take the cart much further. I will seek out a suitable walking stick for you."

"Non, Gaeten, you and Jacques go ahead without me. I will remain here with the burrow. He will appreciate my company."

Gaeten stood back and saw the old man's soul.

"We are not in a race. The crimson bush will be there as long as we wish it to be. The achievement will be that we make it to the rock together. You will hop on my back and we go onward."

Old Mansart's body sagged with fatigue, but his spirits soared to remain part of the adventure.

"Jacques, you can make a sling from this fabric," Gaeten said. "Once Old Papa is on my back, pass the corners to me and I will tie it off at the front."

"Oui, Papa, one time Mama showed us how the Micmacs make their papoose. Old Papa, you will like riding in a papoose."

When the noon sun was at its highest overhead, Jacques shrieked, "I see it . . . the crimson bush!"

"It's incredible!" Old Mansart shouted, peering over his son's shoulder. "I have never seen such a sight."

"It is exactly as da Vinci envisioned," Gaeten said.

With new energy, the party advanced toward the rocky ridge. Jacques ran ahead to find the portal to the caverns oblivious to his thorny wounds, he tore at the briar bushes.

"Jacques, slow down, there is an order to be respected. The opening is a sacred place where great men have passed. We must show honor before we intrude."

"Oui, Papa. I almost forgot to tell you . . . late one night, an elderly man whispered in my ear. He said I was chosen for great things and that I must use my curiosity."

Gaeten was at a loss as the seers had denied any interference with Jacques without Gaeten's approval. "What did this man look like and where did he come from?"

"Ancient, but kind and gentle. Mama would have described him as mythical. He came out of the darkness and was gone before I could open my eyes, but I remember his words."

Laying old Mansart on a grassy knoll to watch, Gaeten and Jacques prepared to enter the cavern. The boy stopped and raised his hand.

"Listen! I hear humming, but something more. Do you hear purring and swishing, Papa?"

C'est Ickty and Leviathan. Do I dare to believe again?

Watching his son's thrill of adventure, a sensation overcame Gaeten. Knowing he could not squeeze through the opening, Jacques' time had come to be the adventurer.

"I will watch from here, Jacques. Tell me what you see as you advance."

Look at me, I am as the seers were to me when they first sent me into the caverns, listening and peering from the entrance.

Gaeten oiled the lantern and struck the flint. "This will light your path. Do not be afraid, but expect to encounter strange beings . . . they are my old friends. The talisman in your hand will protect you."

As the boy disappeared inside, Gaeten pressed his ear to the crevice and heard every footstep. Jacques' voice echoed to him from within.

"It is wet, Papa, and has a small creek. The walls trickle with water, but I see a dim light ahead. The purring and humming are louder now."

As if Jacques' heart was pounding in his own chest, Gaeten felt he could hardly breathe. He desperately wished he could be there with his son.

The lad's voice called out with excitement. "I see a den of gigantic bones as in a grave pit. And I hear purring or snoring. What if I awaken your Leviathan? What do I do, Papa?" The echo repeated until the words ceased.

"Let him come to you. Show your curiosity but that you mean no harm. The serpent-dinosaur, Levi, only spews fire to defend himself when he is frightened. Let him smell you and breathe into his nostrils. He is lonely and craves a friend."

Gaeten listened for a reply for what seemed an eternity but instead heard the humming of an offen.

"Ruskin, my friend, are you with Jacques?"

His voice echoed inside until Gaeten heard the hoot of an owl, then flapping and cawing with distant chatter.

"I heard those sounds when Ruskin came to the crew's rescue in the maple bush."

Closing his eyes he was aware that his thought had been transported to Jacques' location. He was astounded to realize that he had the vision of a seer.

"Dragons and nymphs live forever, but little boys grow into men and take on responsibility. I will forever believe in my inner strengths and the magic the world has to offer. I wish all of this for Jacques."

"Ahoy! Is there a mariner out there?" Ruskin called from within.

"Yes, come out to share your secrets and discovery."

"Gaeten, I have permission from the seers that four of us will come out now to celebrate this accomplishment and we'll frolic in the sunshine."

"Four!"

Gaeten ran to carry Old Mansart closer. "Dear Papa, you are about to see the most wondrous event of your lifetime. Don't question it but let your heart believe."

First Jacques emerged, then the serpent-dragon Levi, batting beautiful eye greens as the sun struck his vision. Next was the flapping, cooing dinosaur-bird Ickty, followed by his old nymph friend, Ruskin.

Gaeten stroked the two prehistoric beasts and whispered of his fond memories. Old Mansart was speechless watching it, and Jacques was enthralled with the reunion and the intensity of emotion.

"Oh, Papa, thank you for this, that I have seen from my heart the beauty that God has provided me if only I believe which I do. I am honored to be chosen for this adventure."

The old man was paralyzed at the moment, but a deep yearning forced him to get up and wobble on his peg leg advancing toward the beasts.

"When you were a wee babe yourself, Gaeten, I heard of the magical dragon in the hills. Every boy longs to have a majestic pet such as these. One day while lying on the grass and watching the clouds pass overhead, I heard flapping above. I am convinced now … what I saw that day was this wonderful flying beast you call Leviathan."

Jacques tugged at his father's arm. "Can I fly with them, Papa? Leviathan will keep me safe."

Gaeten pondered it as he patted Ickty and Leviathan while they cooed and purred.

Whispering in their ears he spoke to the depths of their souls until he felt the same oneness he had with Ickty over the Huron village.

"Oui, Jacques, the dinosaurs and dragons are most joyful when they are with children and friends. But you will need to hold tight and trust them."

Levi's eyes lit up and his body grew and wiggled as Gaeten gave the reins of his dinosaur friends to his son.

Ickty lowered his head and sat on Gaeten's shoulder and began to purr and whimper.

"Old Papa, he is asking you to come too."

Old Mansart stood up as tall as possible. "I will be so proud to be part of this magic. I will not even blink unless I miss a flap of a wing or a soar of the neck."

"Merci, Old Papa, you remind me that no matter what my age may be, it is the belief and magic in my heart."

Jacques nestled into Leviathan's neck, and Gaeten sat behind with Ickty proudly on his arm. Old Mansart, in his papoose, wrapped his arms around his son's girth.

Flying over Limoilou, they laughed at the miniature sights of the town, with faces looking skyward. Over Limoilou, they dipped to coast past Catherine and Charlotte, waving and calling from the garden.

Soaring over the coastline, Gaeten's and Jacques' hearts beat as one. Levi spread his florescent wings wide and Ickty closed his eyes in euphoria.

For years later, tales were told across France of the magical dragons of Limoilou. Jacques became familiar with the glowing doorknob and old Mansart was welcomed into taverns to tell pirate stories.

Gaeten remained in his quest for knowledge, and when they were ready, he took Jacques and Charlotte on a ship to the Micmac village to see the new world where their mother's ancestors thrived.

The people of Saint-Malo would always remember the legends of Gaeten Mansart and the magical dinosaurs. Long after the offen village had been overgrown, tales and legends of the little people continued in the taverns.

When boys and girls of Saint-Malo frolicked on the beaches and hillsides, their visions claimed reports of a flying dragon overhead, with laughing children on its back. Spellbinding legends were told for generations to follow.

The End

If you enjoyed BOY FROM SAINT-MALO, you might like the many short chronicles in my 620 page historical fiction.

HOMAGE: CHRONICLES OF A HABITANT
A ten generation historical fiction, in a series of short chronological stories, beginning in France in the 1600s. A 500 year journey based on a family's lives, tragedies and immigration to North America. Experience typical life as the early migrants travel from France to settle in Quebec, with generational conflicts and cultural clashes in the founding of the new land.